Katharine Tynan

A Cluster of Nuts

Being sketches among my own people

Katharine Tynan

A Cluster of Nuts
Being sketches among my own people

ISBN/EAN: 9783337097141

Printed in Europe, USA, Canada, Australia, Japan

Cover: Foto ©Andreas Hilbeck / pixelio.de

More available books at **www.hansebooks.com**

A CLUSTER OF NUTS

BEING

SKETCHES AMONG MY OWN PEOPLE

BY

KATHARINE TYNAN
(Mrs. H. A. HINKSON)

" Kindly Irish of the Irish,
Neither Saxon nor Italian."

LONDON
LAWRENCE & BULLEN
16, HENRIETTA STREET, COVENT GARDEN, W.C.
1894

Many of these sketches have already appeared in the "Speaker," the "Westminster Gazette," the "Weekly Sun" and the "Monthly Packet," to the editors of which I am under obligation for the first favour of their publication and the second of permitting me to republish them.

TO

MARY GILL,

FOND AND ENDURING FRIENDSHIP.

MO CRAOIBHIN CNO.*

The Irish woods have sycamore and quicken,
  Chestnut and beech and elm-trees set a-row;
And in the hazel copse the clusters thicken—
      Mo craoibhin cno !

In the green hazels play the squirrel people,
  Bright-eyed and brisk, not fearing any foe,
As safe above the world as daw in steeple,
      Mo craoibhin cno !

The nuts are sweeter to the dainty squirrels
  Than garden-fruit or blackberries aglow ;
Sweeter than to the youth his brown maid's curls—
      Mo craoibhin cno !

I wandered by the hazels ere they withered,
  And heard the blackbird's liquid numbers flow ;
And from the bough a cluster brown I gathered—
      Mo craoibhin cno !

Russet and small, but still within the brownness
  May hide some sweetness—pray you find it so !—
As pleases squirrels in the old wood's loneness—
      Mo craoibhin cno !

Brown nuts, my masters, from an Irish hazel !
  But if ye will not their rough flavour, go
And leave my fruit for finer fruits that dazzle—
      Mo craoibhin cno !

* Ma creevin O, *i.e.*, My cluster of nuts.

CONTENTS.

A

CLUSTER OF NUTS.

A VILLAGE GENIUS.

THEY buried him to-day in the green God's Acre sown thickly with human dead, in the shadow of the little church with its square Norman tower, in the longer shadow of the Round Tower, raised so long ago that even its uses and its age are dimly guessed at, and that yet for all its hoariness in the verdant landscape looks Time between the eyes, and defies him, as it did—how many centuries ago ? The Round Tower has seen much of death : many times, no doubt, this rich plain was a battle-field for many races.

One who steals by the churchyard with a
trembling heart might start to realize that
underfoot, no matter whither one wends, there
lie the forgotten dead; for our Old World has,
every inch of it, been honeycombed with
graves. The Round Tower stands in the
smiling landscape like a Sphinx holding its
secrets and its thoughts. Of a summer
afternoon it sets its long shadow like the
shadow on the dial-plate across the graves.
Tick, tick, goes the clock of Time; if you
listen you hear it in the silence, and Time
passes, and we with it. But the Round Tower
knows that, like the seasons, everything
returns: there is never a lack of golden heads
at the cottage doors; nor birds to sing in the
boughs in spring after the snow and the frost;
nor apple blossoms, though last year's fell in
showers; nor delicate pale leaves, though the
autumn swept such a myriad of dead leaves
down the village street, to creep and whisper
about the feet of the Round Tower like little
ghosts of dead dreams. To the Round Tower

everything returns; and because he is well-nigh eternal, he never notices such a detail as that they are not the same children, or the same birds, or the same blossoms and leaves. But it will not be next year, nor for many a year, that he will again look upon a village genius.

The village genius was the son of a shoe-maker, one of a family of robust brothers, all of the same trade, and himself unwillingly making boots for the farmers while his feet would fain be climbing the hill of Parnassus. I think, however, he was a shoemaker *manqué*; or how else was it that one would meet him sometimes striding along on a frosty afternoon when the setting sun turned all the snow to scarlet? an open book in his hand wherein the dusk was blotting out the letters, his gait a little fierce; striding along, as I have said, as if he would so walk away from something that irked him in his daily life. That was before I knew him so well as I did of late years, before I became his literary guide, and my word his judgment.

He was at the unromantic age of forty-two
when he died ; a spare man, with hair greyer
and thinner than it should have been, regular
pale features, eager eyes that jumped at you
when you gave an advice or an explanation, a
high bulging brow that might have given
warning of the brain disease he was to die
from.

His life had had many disappointments. His
own family were not untender, but were somewhat impatient of him ; they wanted him to be
a good shoemaker, not a bad poet.   The people
among whom he lived smiled at his ambitions,
not realizing how much more ignoble were
their own : his aspirations and dreams were to
the world he lived in nothing like so poetically
named a thing as a midsummer madness.   He
had a sweetheart once, a hypocritical meek-
faced thing, a village coquette with a pure
profile, and hidden eyes, and pale soft cheeks
under her drooping ringlets. She led the
village genius into Paradise, and walked with
him in its paths for a little while ; then she

jilted him shamefully and shamelessly, for a
friend of his, a good earner, troubled with no
useless dreams and visions. They went to
America, and the village genius gave no second
woman the chance of wounding him.

Henceforth his devotion was to his lady
Literature. Devotion more profound and
entire I have never known. So long as he
touched the hem of her skirt he was satisfied.
He did wonders considering his difficulties.
He made his way to France and remained long
enough to learn the language, so as to get at
the French writers. He had dreams of going
further afield, especially when in latter days he
grew prosperous ; but, alas ! his feet will never
again wander from his own village.

The first essays in literature he brought to
me would have made me smile if he had not
been so deeply in earnest. He had read only
the stately, old-fashioned writers, the essayists
of the *Spectator*, the poetry of Pope, who was
his favourite. Add to the formality thus
acquired the Irish peasant's love for big and

sonorous words, and imagine the result! From the first I took him in earnest, and he was very docile. I preached to him perpetually the doctrine of simplicity. It was not easy to persuade him that it was better to say a thing was "red" than it was "of ruby dye," but little by little he learned, and was encouraged as his simple verses became acceptable to a newspaper, now and again. Then his subjects : he was quite capable at the time of a Dantesque poem on the Last Judgment, or another Ode on the Nativity. But by degrees he accepted my dictum that he must only write of things he knew, and so he came in time to write sketches of the life about him, with a certain vigorous realism, and to make simple verses on familiar things which, with every trial, came nearer to being poetry. I can see him sitting before me now, in his shoemaker's leather apron, as he sometimes came early in the morning, waiting with his eager eyes upon me as I read his latest story or verse, and sensitively ready to wince if my judgment were adverse. I often looked at him, indeed more in sorrow than in anger, for it was not easy to keep him from relapsing into magnificence, and verses opening delicately and sweetly would pull up about the third verse with a burst of bathos. However, I think I helped him every time he came, and he used to go away happy, his arms, with the turned-up sleeves, often full of the overflow from my book-shelves. He was an ascetic genius—in life and in his mind. He never touched drink ; and in even the innocent pleasures of those about him he had no part : so he was attracted in litera-ture by a chilly excellence, and had little feeling for colour or passion.

Those realistic stories of his often brought him into ill-repute. They were literal tran-scripts from the life about him, and when a paper drifted into the village containing a photographic description of how the Widow S—— behaved to her husband in life and when he lay dead, or a certain curious page in the early family history of the most prosperous person in the village, there was commotion.

But the village genius heeded it no more than the battle of the frogs that made all the water tremble in a deep ditch he passed on his evening walk towards the hills. If they thought him an unprofitable, and now a scurrilous person, he was too remote from them to heed. He lived in a world of his own ; when he was hammering boots on the shop bench and his thoughts were withdrawn into himself; when he sat in his bedroom in the roof among his books, and opened his high window to the stars ; when he paced towards the mountains in a mood of exaltation that marked their solemnity and their eternal peace, but overlooked their transcendent colouring. I fear the village genius had a certain arrogance for his surroundings, and that as he found his expression, these people amongst whom he was bred and born became only so much material to him.

The stories led up to the season of prosperity of which I have spoken. His stories and his sketches became acceptable to a couple of papers which were connected. One was a Society paper of the most vapid sort, more foolish if less vicious than its London proto- types. To this the village genius not only con- tributed stories and sketches, but also Society paragraphs, for his sister had gone away and become a *modiste* to the great world, by which it will be seen that he was not the only remark- able person of his family. I often thought the editor of that Society paper was a bold man, for the genius drew on the long memories of the old people around him as well as his own, and many a strange page in the histories of county families found its way into the Society paper thinly disguised. The village genius con- tributed much to the paper for some time before he died, and I often smiled, seeing it in the hands of fashionable dames and misses, over another vision of the village genius in leather apron and with grimy face and hands. He felt it as a somewhat ignoble prosperity, but he was proud to earn money by the pen so long derided, very proud to draw out with

pretended unostentation a cheque for his
literary services, in full sight of his brothers
and his fierce old father, who had raged against
the piles of useless manuscript and the feckless
son who would spend good sixpences by stealth
to procure the *Athenæum* or the *Saturday
Review*.

Yet, apart from this sordid gain, he kept a
pure aspiration, and worked at his little poems
by night, and strove patiently in his 'prentice-
ship to the art he hoped some day humbly to
learn. It is all over now, and the rain will
beat to-night above his quiet face. The
little hard buds are forming on the trees,
and the green snowdrop spears pushing
sturdy heads above-ground; even in the damp
days there is a fresh breath of spring that
sets all the birds to chattering. But he
is heedless of it all, and the lovely and
ordered procession of the months that once
delighted him will pass him unheeded At
last he lies quite close to the heart of nature
and the secret of all things. To him patiently

learning, might have been said, in the exquisite
words of a modern poet :—

> " Wait, and many a secret nest,
> Many a hoarded winter store,
> Will be hidden on thy breast.
> Things thou longest for
> Will not fear or shun thee more.
>
> Thou shalt intimately lie
> In the roots of flowers that thrust
> Upwards from thee to the sky,
> With no more distrust
> When they blossom from thy dust.
>
> Silent labours of the rain
> Shall be near thee, reconciled ;
> Little lives of leaf and grain—
> All things shy and wild
> Tell thee secrets, quiet child."

In life he would scarcely have had ear for the
subtle sweetness of such poetry, yet it makes
my thought of him, lying where the graves
crowd thickly towards human sympathy and
the occasional footfall of the living. The
Round Tower knows the secrets of the upper
air, but the quiet dead

> " Fear no more the heat o' the sun
> Or the furious winter rages,"

at rest in the earth amid the growing things, and in hope of a glorious immortality. There the village genius has learned masterfully intimacy with familiar things, and the last great simplicity of death.

WAYFARERS.

AT Limerick Junction we first heard it, the indescribable wail, rising and falling, terrible as the "keen" for the dead, which means the farewell of the emigrants. We were quite out of the station at the end of a long train, and it was my travelling companion told me what it meant. A country train laden with emigrants and their friends had come in, and they were parting here, the emigrants coming on with us to Queenstown. No wonder they wailed, one thought, looking away, and trying to forget it. The rain was over, and the Galtees had sailed royally out of the mist; Galtymore, that is the home of eagles, holding his head so high, that I remembered how an imaginative child once took him to be the throne of God. Below the tall peaks ran a rampart of dark blue—a frowning natural fortification behind which lies Aherlow, the fairest of glens, with woolly catkins on the willow boughs, and drifts of primroses among the uncurling ferns, and the mountains all around grey as glass, or red and brown like a pheasant's breast, or streaked along the surface with the blue and green of the peacock, or again, towards evening flushed with roseate light, pulsing from one knew not where. O the dear country, so rich and ready to repay all care! How often they will think of it, when they are nipped to the heart with cold, or are dying of the heat as cruel! How they will long for this cool green, full of dew and scent, and this wind that comes across the mountains, bracing as an air for giants! They will see the cattle going home so gently along the young grass, and hear the Angelus-bell in their dreams, ringing so peaceful and holy from a distant belfry. But down at Queenstown there is the big ship for them, puffing like a grampus out near the forts; and as they sail away

between those gates out into the world, they
will leave behind them more than the unforget-
table country they will never see again.

As the train steamed off, my travelling-com-
panion leisurely opened a violin-case beside
her, and began touching the strings. She was
a little woman, young and pretty,—married, I
discovered from the good-looking fellow who
had seen her off at Dublin—the brownest of
brunettes, with two rows of little white teeth,
and the brownest eyes I have ever seen in a
human face. She talked delicious Cork, with
a soft wail. She was dressed very prettily in
artistic colours that brought out her dear
brownness. Her music and her books made
us conversation, and I found that though she
hailed from the Ultima Thule to which she
was returning, she was very much of the best
part of the world and its ways, thoroughly up
to the last new thing in books and pictures and
music. I congratulated myself on such a companion in my third-class carriage, for in Ireland
people of very small pretensions indeed disdain

to travel third-class, and it is usually left to the roughs.

At the first station we stopped at there was a sound of argument in the first-class carriages close by. Then our carriage door was opened, and a couple of men were unceremoniously pushed in, their bundles thrust after them, and the train started on its way. One was a middle-aged man, grey for lack of good living, but the face redeemed from grimness by the most innocent blue eyes, wide open, candid, blue as a child's eyes. He stumbled over our feet almost sobbing with excitement, clutching to his breast something wrapped in many folds of paper. He was followed by a tall, gawky young fellow, his son evidently, from the like-ness between them. The young fellow was ruddier but had the same slow seriousness of look, something quiet and heavy and patient, as though they had no occasion for joy and laughter. One could see them incessantly striving to wring a sustenance from stony rock and exhausted soil, incessantly face to face with the wet climate that, though it gives such beauty of cloud and mist, soddens the potatoes and rots the corn and turns the meadow to bitter rank grass.

Both were greatly disturbed. The boy's blue eyes had even a dash of angry tears in them. Dropped into their seats, they talked for a while in Irish that sounded very fierce. One felt a curious lump in the throat for their hurt and anger, whatever it might be; it was as if one saw a child or an animal greatly aggrieved. I saw my little friend in the corner watching them with eyes like brown jewels. I think she knew their Irish, or some of it, for she was plainly more in the secret of what was going on than I. At last the excited talk ceased, and the two faces began to take again that look of grave patience which must have been theirs habitually.

Then I saw her lean over and put a dainty finger on the parcel on the elder man's knee.

" Have you no case for your fiddle ? "

c

she said, "Won't the damp get in and spoil it
as it does mine?"

"Spoil her, me lady!" said the man,
brightening all over his face, "is it spoil her?
Och, then, she'd take a power of spoilin', that
same fiddle. 'Tis she that knows the hard
weather. She's a fine fiddle," he said, preparing to display "her"; "she'd put the
joy in your heart and the spring in your
heels at a weddin' or a pattern, but it's at
home she's at her best, and many a night
she's made Thady here and me forget our
throubles."

The fiddle was carefully lifted out, and three
interested heads bent over it, for Thady had
joined the conclave. There was a string gone,
and my friend volunteered one from her store.
While she was arranging it, her soft talk and
sympathy got at the trouble we had seen
without understanding. As I watched her, the
peasant's old fiddle on her knee, while she
tuned and strung it, and resined the bow, the
two men bent forward, gazing at her manipula-

tion of it with almost incredulous pleasure. I said to her silently,—

"Well, my dear, whoever you are, the fairies gave you the gift to make men happy. There may be prettier women and wittier women, but the men who love you will find other women unpleasing to come after you."

"An' so, me lady," the elder emigrant was saying, " me an' Thady, that never travelled a mile from Adeelish before, we just got into the grand cushioned carriage as the train was goin'. An' thin we saw a lady, or a woman dressed grand, for she was no lady like you, me lady, sittin' in the corner starin' at us as if we were the dirt under her feet.

" ' Do ye know,' she says, with the sparks flashin' from her eyes. 'that ye're in the first class ? '

" ' Well, me lady, me and Thady didn't want to inthrude,' and we were about to spake her fair when she burst out,—-

" ' An' I'll have yez removed by the guard at

the very next station, yerselves an' your dirty
baggage.'

"Well, me lady, I could have answered her
bitther enough, but me heart was too heavy for
it, and sure it's a short world to be fightin' in,
so I said nothing; only Thady, that's young
an' fiery, he says, 'It's no baggage, it's
luggage.'

"'Baggage it is,' says she, 'an' out you and
it shall go.'

"Well, I just kept the boy quiet—for what's
the use of arguin' with a beggar a-horseback
like that ?—and so we said nothing, while she
looked out of the window sniffin', as if the sight
of us would make her sick.   An' so when we
came to Emly, we were just putting together
our bits of things to get out, when she runs to
the window an' calls 'Porter!' in a great flurry,
an' complains of me an' the boy travellin' first-
class.

"The porter just spoke her civil, though I
saw him winkin' at another porter, an' so we
got out ; but before I could reach back for the

darlin' fiddle, she comes and pitches it out on
the window, an' when it fell I thought it was
flesh and blood. The boy here was for pullin'
out her own fine portmanty; an' as for me, all
the blood was in me head, but, glory be to God!
the porters pulled us away an' there was no
harm done. An' she's no worse for the fall
ayther, for she was well swathed around. An'
sure it was great good luck, after all, that put
us in with such a kind lady as yourself."

My little friend was as much excited over
the story as the actors in it. The way she
entered into their pathetic indignation at their
bundles being called "baggage," which they
evidently took to be a term of contempt, was
wonderful. Her eyes flashed, and a bit of
scarlet came in her brown cheeks as she
denounced the fastidious first-class passenger
almost with tears of anger. When the commotion was all over, she asked to hear "her,"
and first the father and afterwards the son
performed on the poor instrument, jigs, reels,
planxtys, giving way slowly to mournful Irish

lamentations. After they had gone through their *répertoire*, Brown Eyes produced her fine fiddle, and, in accordance with delicately urged entreaties, began to play. It was a fine instrument, and a fine hand upon it, and the music at first was from the great masters ; then, having dazzled her audience a little, she began to play Irish airs—" The Coolun " and " The Blackbird " and others—while the tears rolled down the faces of the two emigrants.

We were nearly at Cork when the musician came out of her dream. If I ever saw adoration on the faces of human beings, it was on those simple faces. They will talk of her for years and years I am sure. She was consistently gracious, and after they had thanked her and she them, with the prettiest of Irish com- pliments on each side, they were preparing to put the treasure in its wrappings when the little lady said, " Oh, but your fiddle would be destroyed by the sea-air, and you could never play on her again in America, you know. Now, I'll get a case in Cork, and you'll make me happy if you'll accept this old case." And so "she" was put to sleep in a velvet-lined case such as she had never dreamt of in all her hardworking life.

After we had gone through the long tunnel and emerged in gay sunlight at Cork, she stood up to leave us. She bowed to me with pretty courtesy, but to the emigrants she held out her little hands. The two big fellows dropped down and kissed them as if she were a saint. "God bless an' keep you," said the father; " we'll think of you in America when we play the fiddle. 'Tis you God made for a lady, an' to be the light of some one's eyes; and the man that loves you, you'll keep his love while fire burns an' water runs."

There was a flash of answering tears in her eyes, and she was gone down the platform, her velvet hat pulled forward a little, and daintily graceful in her hooded brown velvet cloak. She passed the first-class passenger, whom I recognized by the emigrants' sullen references, though, indeed, she "jumped to the eye" by her vulgarity. A couple of apple-women pointed delightedly at this arrogant dame, and one spat out expressively. My poor emigrants dropped into gloom after their benefactress left them, and they looked grey and sad enough, despite the new fiddle-case, by the time we reached Queenstown, where the big liner was steaming heavily near the quay.

A COUNTRY AUCTION.

THE frost was come to stay, every one declared, for the snow long threatening had rolled up his wool-packs and betaken himself and them to the North Pole. The air was windless and bitterly cold; the sun had gone down in a haze of scarlet. Now the frost was sending up fingers of scarlet in the west sky, shining redly in every steely car-track on the road, faintly flushing the silvery sprinkle of powdered snow on the fields; throwing up in delicate relief against a sky of rose and sapphire the exquisite outlines of the bare branches. The ground was imprinted on its light snow with the delicate foot-prints of the birds, and the hoofs and paws of beasts.

All day folk had flocked to the house on foot, or, despite the iron-bound roads, by car

from the city. Country people grumbled because the frost had not kept the town buyers
at home. Frowsy dealers filled the rooms
with an atmosphere of old clothes and un-
washed humanity, cursed openly the auctioneer's flowery advertisement that had
brought them so far on a fool's errand,
handled carelessly and contemptuously the
old woman's treasures, and finally departed,
to the great sweetening of the air. All day
the crowd had tramped from room to room,
nothing being sacred to them, had discussed
and appraised, had squabbled over lots, and
defiled, with feet on which the snow was
melting, floors that had shone as white and
silvery as sand and scrubbing could make
them.

It was a generous, ancient, comfortable
house, stretching itself brown in the sun and
the fields—the very house to shelter troops of
merry children, lads and lasses, God-fearing
happy people in their prime, old men and
women ageing sweetly and venerably. It had

been built by a rich young husband of long
ago as a country house for his fine-lady wife ;
but she, being urban and genteel, and the
place lonely, sighed for the city, away there in
blue mist, the roar of whose not over-con-
gested traffic rumbles here on the sea-wind.
So the doting husband shut up his mansion,
and the place grew old in loneliness ; and,
never the foster-mother it looked, gazed from
its height with a more than human melancholy.
The sweet old garden was overgrown ; rose
and gooseberry, parsley and pansy, all in
wild tangle. The rabbits burrowed among
the stocks, the blackbirds helped themselves
daintily to cherries in season, the slugs ate the
strawberries, and in autumn the damsons fell
like a mournful purple blight among the yellow
plums. Now and then little cottage children
made a tiny raid, but on the very outskirts,
for the poor house, long untenanted, had
gained an evil repute, and they feared they
knew not what horror gazing upon them from
the barred, unshuttered windows.

The old woman had taken away some of its reproach.   The rooms she inhabited she made clean with an ancient habit of industry, polishing the brown shutters and panels till they reflected things, and the brass lining of the fireplaces till they winked again.   She set up in them her solid, respectable furniture— bureaux and bookcases made in the days when furniture was fashioned, not for time, but eternity; clock-faces that clicked away the hours with a deliberateness which seemed to make time never-ending; old-fashioned engravings in solid frames; china, brown and quaint; Waterford glass, heavy as rock crystal.   She sat among them on a Sunday afternoon, drinking her tea of unparalleled strength and fragrance, and reading a weekly paper, whereof the entertaining paragraphs gave her a quite sufficient outlook into the affairs of the world.   Other days she toiled as unremittingly as though daily bread had to be obtained; on Fridays she jolted on her side-car to the city, drew what money she needed from the bank, added perhaps to the store which was to buy her another three per cent. debenture, and jogged home again, pleasantly tired from her outing. Her one extravagance in all the years was a sealskin coat, which she sported at the early mass one June Sunday, and then relegated as too precious to be worn to tissue paper and camphor. A lonely old woman, with her two brothers in the churchyard, and for kin a crowd of unknown folk whom she would not let pass her door, and whose fingers itched greedily for her consols and her land; derided and cheated by her work-people, grown too hard in long getting of money to keep even her dreams—her dreams of the brown-faced ambitious lover she rejected in her youth at her elder brother's command. The heart that had been hers was long ago ashes in the earth; the husband that might have been, and the children that might have been, vanished into the great limbo: the story of him meant more to a young, sympathetic listener hearing it from his contemporary,

than to her who in her youth had broken
his heart.

The lots were nearly all sold, and the crowd
had made acquaintance with every nook and
corner, except the drawing-room, big enough
for a ball, which was long shuttered and silent,
the home of spider and mouse, and the kitchen,
where the gray-faced heir-at-law had hid himself, being ungenial. He was busy, no doubt,
musing on his £20,000 of Government securi-
ties, and his twice as much buried in fertile
and kindly land. People enjoyed themselves
highly pulling old-world things into the light:
no one had compunction; not the round-
faced priest, with his rosy cheeks dimpling to
ready laughter, nor the country gentleman in
knickerbockers, with a fine collie at his heels,
nor the young farmer's wife, alert for crockery
and napery, and quivering with excitement
when the selling came near the object of her
desire. There was not one there had a
thought of love or of pity for the dead
woman, though many sighed virtuously over

the accumulation of things, and with vicarious
charity wished they might have been sold and
given to the poor.

The dead woman may have turned in her
grave at the last scene of all. People were
grouped outside in the cold slush to see the
sale of the old woman's wardrobe. The things
had been kept in her bedroom upstairs in a
silent air of lavender and camphor. From the
upper window the auction took place to great
advantage. First there were bundles of house-
linen, old and yellow and fine, gathered with
God knows what girl's dream of home and
love. Then there were some pitiful things—a
beaver hat of the forties, which had belonged
to one of the dead brothers ; a sprigged waist-
coat with blue stars on a black velvet ground ;
an old coat of bottle-green cloth, many-
pocketed and brass-buttoned. As it flapped
forlornly from the upper window the crowd
screamed with delight, and the auctioneer's
clerk, snub-nosed and impudent, who had re-
placed his tired-out master at this the fag-end

of the sale, was in his happiest vein of humour.
When the men's clothes had all been disposed
of, there came a couple of delicate Indian
shawls, slightly moth-eaten, yellow with years,
worth their weight in gold to a connoisseur,
but mere caviare to this crowd. I had them
for a song. Then came the old woman's
gowns. As a preliminary to their sale, the
auctioneer's clerk set astride his impudent
face with its red beard a cottage bonnet,
purple and white ribbons on white Dunstable,
in which the dead woman — who to the last
kept her skin of egg-shell china, and her delicate prettiness of feature — may have looked
adorable in the eyes of a lover when the century was still young. Some of the gowns were
very old, as the short skirts, frilled at the foot,
and the baby sleeves and bodices told. From
those cottons and muslins what soft shoulders
and arms may have peeped forth ! Over the
sealskin there was a fierce competition ; but
the ancient things fell by consent to the wives
of the work-people, who were all there enjoy-

ing the show, and finding the witticisms of the
auctioneer's clerk as entertaining as a clown at
the pantomime.

I was hugging my Indian shawls, with their
little ancient air of distinction, and was thinking how they might have graced a fine lady's
shoulders at the Opera, or warmly enwrapped a
precious first baby being carried to the baptis-
mal font, when in language of sumptuous
irony the *pièce de résistance* of the old woman's
wardrobe was introduced. " Somethin' ultra-
choice," said the brazen voice, " for it has as
many peels on it as an onion, an' by all accounts is such as any lady might wear walkin'
out with her beau." And then came out of
silver paper a modest quaint old gown, evidently matched with the Dunstable, a delicious
frilled thing of shot purple and white, made
with elaborate hangings of fringe, and a
spencer to cross a modest bosom. The
empty laughter seemed shocking, for somehow I guessed it was a wedding-dress, and,
wrapped away in it, I conjectured a dead

D

youth, a dead love, hopes that had had no
fruition, desires that were dust and ashes.
So there was a touch of sentiment in the old
woman, after all.   As the thing flapped by its
hanging sleeves, a sweet old odour drifted to
my nostrils.   The others were too tickled in
ears and eyes to have another sense on the
alert.   It seemed a horrible profanation, and it
made one grind one's teeth at the inheritor of
the old woman's wealth who had not saved her
from this. She had been well-loved by her two
brothers—the elder, who had made her what
she was because she was too dear to be given
to another man, the younger, who had outlived
him and leant upon her stronger nature in his
last years of later middle age.   She had been
well-loved by the man she had rejected, who
had never put another in the place she had
laid waste.   They were all work-a-day folk,
but there was a time when the passion of any
one of the three would have leaped out to
avenge a rough word to her.   Now they were
mouldering quietly while her most secret

things were jibed at with callous indecency. Alas! for the patient dead, and alas! for the husbandless and childless woman, who has been of little account from the days of Holy Writ down to the last comic opera of Messrs. Gilbert and Sullivan. The wedding-dress that had never been worn fell to some dealer in old clothes, and was carried off on her arm, forlornly hanging, with a suggestion of a limp human shape, like one of Bluebeard's wives suspended in a closet.

The auctioneer's clerk locked the desolate rooms, gathered up his papers, and joined his master for their cold drive to the city. The heir-at-law followed them. Gay groups were going home by the lanes to bright fires and good food, chattering, laughing, comparing their bargains with each other. The thin Christmas moon wheeled into the sky, with Orion and Arcturus, Venus and Mars, in cloth of silver, to attend her. The house was lonely again, gaunt against the vivid black sky, and full of mysterious sadness. There in the cold

night it looked indeed haunted.   One hurried
away from it, half fearing to see behind the
blank windows the old woman in her grave-
clothes, going from one to the other of her
ransacked hiding-places, discovering one after
another her losses, moaning and wringing her
pale hands because they had taken away from
her her treasures.

A HOUSE OF ROSES.

I KNOW of no lonelier spectacle than that of an old married couple without children.

When youth and health and beauty are here it may matter less, according to temperament; the most lover-like husbands and wives among young married folk of my experience are childless. But when they have grown old, and bent, and withered, how lonely they are for want of a staff, for some one to close the eyes of that most lonely one—the survivor of the two. It must give an added pang to death, for the one that goes leaves the other desolate indeed.

My old lover of roses and his wife were less unhappy than those who have never had a child, for somewhere, in earth or heaven, there was a son of theirs. For the old man there was a never-failing spring of hope; for the old

woman there were memories of the child at her
breast, the little one running between the well
and the orchard, the dear school-boy who, for
all his talents, had the child's heart.   It was
twenty years since he had left them in tears.
Eighteen of these had been a long, dreadful
blank of silence.   If he were living now he
might be a bearded man, with his children
about his knees.   But he must have died long
since; died or changed in some dreadful way,
or he never would have let them wait.   Boys
with an unsullied heart, and bright wits like
his, have come ·miserably to shipwreck before
now.   Their old tin-type photograph of him,
beautiful in spite of elementary photography,
shows a face gay and tender, with a certain
fineness of nostril that promised intensity of
feeling.   Such an one outraged and deceived
might take the path that leads to the pit.
Some fragment of a story was blown my way
of one who might have been the old couple's
only son, one dying lonely in a Melbourne
hospital, his face full of sweet and boyish

curves that the hardness of excess had not had time to obliterate. "Not the first man a bad woman sent to the devil," said the surgeon to the friend who told me the story. But if it was the prodigal son he sent no message. He was conscious at the last, and even confidential, but he resolutely refused to communicate with his home. "When people are dead they are better dead," was his speech. I never hinted it to the old people. Why should I ? There was no evidence at all that this castaway was their son. The name was the commonest of Irish names, and my friend, the Australian editor who unearthed the thing for me, warned me against attaching any weight to it. As likely as not the dead man had given a false name. After this I ceased making endeavours to track the son of the simple old people, who would not know how to undertake such a task for themselves. Often indeed, "the dead are better dead."

The old man was the most primitive of farmers—had been I should say, for he farmed

only the rose in days when I knew him. He
had once possessed a small farm, half a hundred
acres of thistly land, from which savour and
strength had long departed. It was handi-
capped by a big mansion, of which the old
couple inhabited a couple of bare rooms. The
land grew its weak hay year after year. There
was never any return made to it. The old man
pottered in the big 'garden, which was luxuriant, as old gardens are, with a wealth of
fruit, and clusters of roses flapping in your
face as you entered any gateway. Those
old mansions with great gardens and shrub-
beries are thick in Ireland, especially near the
metropolis. They were built long ago for
lords, spiritual and temporal, to whose heirs
London is now the town, and English shires
the country.

The day came when the lease fell in, and
they had to leave the place where their son
was born and they had lived their years of
hope. If they had kept the boy with them,
things might have been different; but they

had been ambitious for him, and had given him the best education within their reach. In the pride of his youth he had laughed at the idea of ever making anything of the exhausted land. There was gold to be had in abundance oversea, gold for the picking and mining ; for some new bonanza had been discovered. What did they know of the world, of sin, and temptation, when they let him go? Such things as gambling and wild living, bad women and quarrels for their sake that make men murderers, were as far away from them as a legendary world, for they read little, and the vice at their doors was of a harmless kind enough. At first, good news had come steadily, and money and a small nugget that stands under a glass shade on the chimney-piece. Then the letters ceased suddenly. The woman suffered more than the man, for after a time of suspense that took out of him any possible spring or enterprise, he developed an irrational and joyful hopefulness. She had to put away her tears and motherly forebodings, because it made her husband so angry to see them.

By-and-by it took some such irritation to disturb his placidity. They had changed from the big house soon after the cessation of the letters. The house they went to had long enjoyed the reputation of being haunted. No one had lived in it within memory. It was a gaunt place, on the very edge of the road, narrow, with windows back and front, so that you could see straight through to the trees at the back. It is on the loveliest bye-road, where every flower in its season appears first and vanishes last on the luxuriant hedgerows. Far down one looks through an avenue of splendid old thorns to the blue walls of mountains. The hawthorn is succeeded there by woodbine and wild rose, the latter falling in close exquisite veils of pink and green down to the daisied grass that lines the ditches. The high road, with its shrieking steam tram, runs at right angles to it, but does not disturb the lane's quietness. By contrast it makes this sylvan

world lovelier, for it is pleasant to reflect that
one is a country mouse and yet on such easy
visiting terms with the city.

For all the surrounding beauty, the house
looked irredeemably ugly when the old folk
came to live there. Who could think it would
ever wear the gracious aspect that it does now
when it is absolutely a stack of roses? Gloire
de Dijon, Maréchal Niel, tea roses; roses in all
colours, from tiny, close, white things, nine or
ten on a spray, through all the gamut of yellow,
pink, rose red, and velvety darkness that is
almost black. Never a one passes that way
but stops in delight. The roses are over the
house, and in the beds, but the house ends are
flanked by huge hollyhocks, and there are beds
at the sides where daffodils and hyacinths
flourish in spring; and for shelter there is a
close hedge of sweetbriar, so ravishingly sweet
that I have seen a very noble and intelligent
St. Bernard dog pause with lifted nostrils to
inhale the fragrance. Folk may be incredulous
about this, but I should like them to see this

country-bred dog, looking up with amazed interest when the leaves first open in spring, or following a lark's flight with grave intentness till it is lost in the dazzle. Perhaps he has learnt his ways from humankind. Certainly he is the only dog I have ever known to display this kind of observation.

It was through great love that the once hideous house came to be a rose-tree in full bearing. They were no sooner settled than the old man began to beautify against Patrick's return. At first he was half anxious lest he should come while the place was so ugly, before the green had covered it. Seasons waxed and waned. The roses throve apace, being cared for as no roses ever have been, before or since. In the winter they were swathed in cocoanut fibre and sacking. In the spring and summer there was an incessant round of kindly tasks for the roses' benefit. I used to pass the house every evening, and winter or summer the old man was always there, with spade or watering-pot or big pruning scissors. No doubt the roses

growing so beautiful, blooming every year in a
superb plenty in June, throwing out a sparser
second crop in autumn, comforted him. Yet
he never ceased to listen for a foot, and when
in time he grew very deaf, he would look up
with a startled lightening of the face when a
shadow fell on him at his work. Rover, the
Irish terrier, that had been Patrick's, shared for
a long time in this hopeful and hopeless vigil.
He was a puppy when his young master went
away, but I don't think he ever forgot him.
He lived to a patriarchal age, a solitary dog,
with the care of an old couple on his mind, as
well as the strain of constantly listening for a
long silent footstep. These things steadied
him, even though the village and its tempta-
tions were not a quarter of a mile away. I used
to see him, in his grizzled old age, lying on
a sack near the old man at his work, his
nose on his outstretched paws, his melancholy brown eyes full of wistful thoughts.
He too, grew deaf, listening for the step that
never came. He died and was buried by

the sweet-briar hedge, and they gave him no successor.

Patrick's mother had no illusions about his coming back. With a woman's faith she thought of him ever smiling-eyed, sweet-lipped under an aureole in heaven. She prayed incessantly for him, and thought of Paradise as a place to be thirsted after, where her boy's arms should be for ever clasped around her neck. She kept her thoughts to herself, however, as the years went on. If she cried it was when she was alone, and I think she must have cried a great deal, for she became in time more than half blind, and her eyes have a pale look, as if the colour were washed away. Her wound was never allowed to close. All those twenty years Patrick's place was set at every meal. His room in the roof, that was scented as with attar of roses from the great bush that draped the windows, was always kept ready. There were periodical airings and dustings, but everything was as though a traveller might come any hour of the day or night.

The master of the roses died last year, in the full flush of the rose harvest. He sleeps in a very ancient churchyard close by, with a green, ivy-covered tower, the haunt of martins and swallows, shadowing his grave; across the road is the garden of the Dominicans, where the figures of the white-cowled, white-robed novices give a touch of sanctity to the lovely place. Sometimes a monk comes walking towards one, with the hills for a background, and in a day of serene blue skies and tremulous green boughs, one might dream it mediæval Italy. The church, which is in the centre of the graveyard, is a Protestant church, built long after saints had begun to lay their tired bones to rest there, but the Angelus-bell rings its more intimate message to him lying among his brethren of the old faith.

This year the roses grew a little rank, and with an over-abundance of leaves. They had to live through the fierce weather of last March without their swathings. They are often thirsty, dusty, and languid of evenings when no shower comes silverly walking upon the hills. They will deteriorate year after year, returning gradually to wildness, or getting too weak to open leafy buds. Already they are the prey of the green fly. Since that brown old face, with more wrinkles than I have ever seen, was covered by the coffin-lid, the widow only appears, stealing, a melancholy black figure, to the church of the Dominicans, or to the grave-yard. I often wonder if Patrick's place is still set and his room ready. It was so much a habit with the lonely old woman that it might well continue. But none now listen for a springing footstep on the road, and if Patrick is yet in this world, he had better come, or no one will be left to welcome him.

A BOOK-LOVER.

I WILL describe him for you as he leans over his half-door of a summer's evening, looking across green fields to the blue distance, where presently the lighthouse lamps will set up their revolving lights. The city is down there in the mist. Beyond it, and beyond a strip of blue sea, the islands and the rocky promontory are steeped in rose and grey. He is quite an old chap, with a jolly, round, bullet-head. His keen face is wizened by many lines of laughter. He is whistling jocundly to himself. If you should tempt him across his threshold to a conversation, he will presently, with hands deep in his pockets, break into a comical jig of a few steps, just for the mere fun of it. He comes up so quite readily to my mind's eye out of the mists

E

of nigh a score of years ago. That is my childhood's impression of him, and I have forgotten, or perhaps never knew, the time when he went heavily, with never a jig in his toes and heels.

His house was high enough for a house of two stories, but compromised matters by a loft at each gable-end, ascended by a ladder and leaving the common living-room a wide space of smoke-blackened wall and thatch. In those days, however, there was little of the wall visible for the stacks of books. He had them piled high, here on a rough brown dresser intended for kitchen crockery, there on a primitive arrangement of shelves, suspended by a cord slung through holes in the end of each. He had bought lavishly, if not wisely, at the book-stalls, and at an occasional sale. Where did he get the money? Heaven knows! He was of the class known in Ireland as "dairy boys," irrespective of age. His wages might be eighteen shillings a week. I suppose what other men spent in whisky or tobacco, with him went for books. His wife, a placid, silent woman, never objected to this extravagance of her man. I suppose she thought it was a peaceable diversion, and very desirable, seeing that other men's diversions led to drink, to rows, and misery.

He might be called a book-worm in the sense that the contents of the books, so far as reaching his mind, concerned him but little. If I said he was more intelligent, more bookish than his fellows, I would be wrong. He loved books with an intensity of devotion, but it was because they were books. The fine distinction of *biblia abiblia* never reached him. Equally delightful they were to him were they "Cumming on the Miracles" or a lurid romance of G. W. M. Reynolds. It was to carry them home, to hold them, to feel them, to climb the ladder and add them to the congested shelves ; *that* made the delight.

I don't know where he found the curious taste. Perhaps it was as well it went no further with him than skin-deep of the books.

It is unsafe to be different from your fellows. I once knew a pigeon who took into his head to desert his own kind for human. He was a handsome fellow, too, and of a high and haughty spirit, A veritable anchorite of the desert to the iris-necked maidens of his kind, who came cooing and languishing about him all in vain. He first constituted himself watch-dog of the forge, opposite the kitchen windows, and followed the blacksmith like a dog, but with more respect for himself than has anything canine. He watched the forge jealously, and resented the presence there of anything, human or otherwise, except himself and his adopted master. Even the harmless necessary horses were shod to the time of his incessant pecking at their hoofs. But one day, in seeking to eject an intrusive hen, who had roosted on a pitch-pot, the pair, in the heat of combat, fell in. But this was not Tom's end. We, whom his originality and fearlessness had made friends, took him to the kitchen, and having cleansed him to the best of our power, left Time and his indomitable spirit to complete the cure. Alack, when he was well past convalescence, and in full possession of the kitchen as he had been of the forge, he disappeared one night from the fender where we had left him nodding. Either a passing cat, or our own perfidious one, had made an end of this rare spirit : which proves that a bird should keep his wings, and not step on the earth to be a prey to cats.

However, no one of his own kind resented my old book-lover's hobby. As for us young-sters he was our Mudie. From his shelves we carried off the stories of the thirties, Mrs. Gore's novels, and Mrs. Trollope's, Miss Sewell's, and Miss Ferrier's. G. W. M. Reynolds we devoured in " The Coral Island," a big tome of horrors ; and there was Eugene Sue's " Mysteries of Paris " in three big volumes, with a picture to every two inches of letterpress. Side by side with such coarse food for young imaginations we had Miss

Wetherall in "Say and Seal" and "The Wide, Wide World," and had the good taste to prefer her. We were omnivorous readers, and were little in fear of check, as our reading-room was an overgrown orchard, where it was easy to elude pursuit or capture, and where we were wicked enough to lie low till voices were tired of calling us, and we were left in peace till the owls began to hoot and the moon swung into the delicate green and rosy sky, and the long, long, delicious day was over.

I don't know if the old fellow had read any of his own books, but there were two he held perpetually before us as a fee if we brought back the long-missing members of batches, as a threat of their being withheld from us if we did not supply the same omissions. I think, myself, they were apocryphal, for I hunted the shelves from end to end and never caught a glimpse of them. They were called "Fatherless Fanny" and "A Necklace of Pearls." If he had the books he treasured them away in a safe place, and whether we restored the missing ones or not, we never caught sight of those oft-dangled bribes.

There was Miss Edgeworth too. I think we knew " Belinda " and " Ennui " and the " Absentee " from cover to cover. Odd volumes of Swift he had too. We liked " Gulliver's Travels," but turned away from the uninvitingness of " A Tale of a Tub." Our indiscriminate reading, after all, did us but little harm. A child desires a story beyond all things, and will turn away from anything that is not a story; and even if one has to wade through much undesirable matter to get one's story, it is with a single attention fixed on it that takes in little else.

Those were good days for the book-lover, and for us, his clients. It was always summer, or the winters have escaped my memory. A milestone of a pantomime stands out in relief now and then, but nothing else at all of the winter. Only for ever the long, long days, and the apples, and the books that one read, devouring apples all the while from one's pinafore with the appetite of some little wood creature.

As well as his wife, there was a daughter in the old book-lover's house; an unexpected girl of her class, as he was a man. Not that she had gifts of any kind, but she was pretty in a delicate way. She was a feather-headed, innocent creature, tall and slender. The old mother did the household work, and Polly's hands were as white as a lady's. Her face was a soft, delicate pink; not rosy and white, but just as faintly pink as a little rose. Round her small head her light, tow-coloured hair stood out as fluffily as if some one had been blowing through it. She, often enough, was leaning over the half-door, looking up and down the road, when we sailed in sight, young pirates, in quest of the books we were so careless about restoring. I don't think she ever did work more serious than making up the muslins and prints that she affected; and that helped to give her that airy look as if

one might blow her away like thistledown.
She was so innocent she often came with us
children mushroom-hunting or blackberry-
gathering. I remember, in a dim way, her
pretty, vacant laughter ; for despite her eighteen years she was as young as the youngest
baby that would not be left at home, though
its company was such a clog and embarrass-
ment. We used to go over hills of furze,
where strange, beautiful little moths fluttered,
blue as the skies, golden-brown, silver. Polly,
in her green or pink muslin frocks, was as
light and fluttering. I don't know where they
have gone to, those moths—whether they
came out of Fairyland and flew back there—
but I never see them now, nor the poisonous
toadstools that grew in brilliant rings of
scarlet, bronze and azure, under the mysterious trees of a park, where now-a-days the
noon is commonplace.

Children notice much, half consciously.
Anyhow, the time came when we knew that
Polly had a lover. We met them sometimes

in the green twilight, when the bats were out ; or when we were selecting our tale of books, Polly languidly looking on, a whistle would come from outside, and Polly, with an increased shade of pinkness, would glide through the doorway, and we saw her no more.

He was a young farmer—much more than Polly's social equal ; he would have called himself a young gentleman, I dare say, having been to boarding-school, and enjoyed other advantages. He was not especially prosperous at the time, for my father had just bought the land which belonged to him and his brothers, and which had been groaning under a weight of debt. There was money enough, however, when divided, to afford each of them a hopeful start in America. By degrees they all did sail for that Eldorado of Irish folk, and prospered, for so long as we knew anything of their doings.

Polly's love affair lasted during a summer. It is like brushing the dust off things in a long-closed room to piece my memories of it. I re-

member a wet August evening when we came
upon them under an overhanging roof of ivy
by a grey wall. The roads were winding
ways of gold with the yellow bind-weed that
flared that summer in long lines, where in
spring there had been an innocent procession
of the daisies. The rain was sweeping silverly
over the hills. The pair were under one
umbrella, Polly's muslin-clad shoulders pro-
tected by a tweed-covered arm that was withdrawn as soon as the little pitchers hove in
sight. They were having merry times; for
before they had seen us we had heard Polly's
laughter, almost violently merry.

Whether her father and mother were anxious
over this unequal love-making I am not sure.
We sometimes came in on conversations
hushed at our entrance. I think our old book-
lover grew disturbed in his heart, for he no
more shuffled into his gay dance, and was
indifferent about the books we took. Judging
by later knowledge, I should think he was
getting afraid his little girl's heart would be

hurt. A coarser fear I am sure he had not. He had the kind of simple refinement that would keep him from wronging in his thoughts the child he had reared with such unusual daintiness. Then she was such an innocent fly-away creature, somehow it would be hard to associate sin with her, or even the serious sorrow and trouble of the world.

A month after that August evening we were caught and caged in school. It had been discovered in some unhappy hour for us that "those children were really running *too* wild." Poor Polly's innocent love story finished itself out after we went. We knew that Polly's Jim was going to America; it was common report. About the time we were getting into the habit of rules and lessons he and his big brothers were on an Atlantic liner. I suppose he was fond of poor Polly in his own selfish way, but not fond enough to marry her. Of course I know nothing about the parting. She was not likely to be very troublesome, poor, tender child, and the old father was too proud to go asking any man to marry her. I suppose they thought she'd forget in time, and once more be happy in the love of the old father and mother, who thought nothing too good for her. However, Polly cut the Gordian knot of her troubles more suddenly.

Another girl, stricken to the heart as she was, would have fallen into a decline and wasted away patiently to the grave. Poor, feather-brained Polly, after a week or so of dull quiet, woke up father and mother one night by talking loudly in a rapid, unnatural voice, broken by bursts of laughter more dreadful still. From the beginning there was no hope. The fever burned and wasted her like wax before the fire. All her pretty hair was cut off, the pink gave way to hectic cheeks and ashen pallor, the pretty rounded-ness grew into sudden sharp curves. On a mild day of October a letter came that told us Polly was dead. When we came home the year after, the old book-lover and his books were gone. When he had laid his little girl to rest he would stay no longer in the place where she had died. He went back to the city—he and his old wife—heavy-hearted, with the books carelessly heaped in a cart. He never came back to see us, as his fellows have always done ; and driving through the city's purlieus, where his home would be, we never caught a glimpse of him. I do not know if he even visits Polly's grave, under the three twisted yews that the west wind has blown awry. The churchyard there abuts on the fields, and is not eerie. The hills look down on it for ever, and the west wind riots above it, and beyond are the fields where Polly walked with her lover twenty long years ago.

HARVESTERS.

I WAS going home for Christmas. It was the long tiresome journey from Euston to Dublin. A too careful porter had bundled me into that abomination—a ladies' carriage—and once installed, I had not taken the trouble to change. What did it matter? I was going home to something so sweet that I and my dreams of it made excellent company, amid which the pleasantest companions one could hope for would be intruders. My fellow-travellers excited in me a less lively curiosity than usual. Yet they were not without interest. The lady with the many babies and nurses had left us at Rugby, amid a general feeling of relief that almost made us friends. There was a forlorn little spinster with mittens, and the *Christian* for her literature. There was the usual fat and comfortable lady, with a frivolous yellow-back and an abundance of sandwiches, which she good-naturedly offered all round. There was an extraordinary little girl who knitted incessantly and wore large round glasses over large round eyes. She was of an amazing self-possession, and when a jolly old gentleman nearly invaded our feminine privacy at Northampton, it was she who stood up, and, pointing with a quivering finger at the inscription on the carriage window, repeated, in a majestic voice, the words, " Ladies only," and so put the intruder to flight. She changed at Chester for somewhere or other, and before she left us graciously regretted that I was not going her way, as I might *have taken care of her.* I was rather abashed at this, feeling my entire unsuitability for such an enterprise ; but replied, I trust, fittingly. Also there were two High Church Sisters, whom I should have taken for Irish nuns, but that they were in charge of a pleasant-looking Anglican clergy-man, who came to look after them at the

stations we stopped at. They dropped their
rosaries through their white fingers, and read
their office, but added nothing to the sociability.
The only other traveller I remember was a soft,
languid, lovely-faced woman, dressed in garments of a country cut, who when she left us
at a Welsh station was received by a gaitered
young farmer, evidently her husband.

"No one for Ireland!" I said to myself,
scanning the faces of my travelling companions.
Out of Ireland one loves all Irish things so
much that an Irish face or voice might have
drawn me from my dreams into sociability.
Irish faces went by the carriage-windows, and
I heard the dear brogue, by fits and starts, at
every station ; but these belonged to men, or
to women in male escort, and happily inde-
pendent of the ladies' carriage.

None of us intruded on each other, save that
detestable little girl. She told us her family
history with great frankness ; and in an interval
between her knitting produced the family
photographs from a woollen reticule, and offere

F

them for our inspection.   I saw the two Sisters smile at each other with a mundane slyness. The comfortable-looking lady put down her Rita novel, and looked amiably at the faded old photographs, and the awful presentments of children of varying ages, with a strong family likeness to our little girl.   Her tide of reminiscences flowed undisturbed till I made a mild joke, which rather put her out.   She was very dogmatic as to the correctness of a little silver watch she carried.   I opined that New-market time—she had told us she came from that sporting town—was sure to be fast.   After this she left me severely alone, and her other listener having brazened it out and returned to her Rita, she was perforce silent.

It was at Crewe we got the Irish reinforce-ment.   It was not such as to please my national vanity.   The train was almost moving when the door was flung violently open, and two Irish harvestmen precipitated themselves into our midst.   I recognized their kind at once; I suppose some extra work had kept them

belated when the rest of their kin had flown
home—when the swallows were flying South,
and the golden wren was flinging herself over
the land's edge on her way to Egypt and the
Pyramids.

They spluttered in mixed Gaelic and English as they righted themselves, and got
seated ; placing their bundles beside them
in the corner seat the shrinking women had
left for them. I eyed them with a cold
disapproval. The first breath sent a whiff
of spirits and coarse tobacco through the
carriage. Their clothes reeked wet and
unwholesome ; the boots of one, the shorter
and stouter of the two, were much in evidence ;
they were unlaced, and he had evidently been
in a cowshed. I saw the little spinster use her
vinaigrette furtively. The matron held her
open book well between her face and them.
The two Sisters were gently disturbed and
unhappy. As for the little girl, the words,
"Ladies only !" had frozen on her lips, and she
was gazing at them with round eyes of objec-

tion.   I felt bitter against those poor country-
men of mine for cutting such a figure in
English eyes.   It was not quite a mean feeling.
My bitterness was in proportion to my love of
native land, and my impatience of English
superiority.

I looked at the two, confounding them in a
common indignation. The elder man, if I had
had but eyes to see it, had a certain dignity.
He had the cavernous dark eyes, the olive skin,
and the unspeakably mournful look of the
Galway peasant. His companion was low-
browed, red-haired, stubby-bearded, with little
red-brown eyes incessantly twinkling, and a
barbarous laugh. He chattered Gaelic to his
quiet companion, interspersing it with loud
spluttering laughter. He spat on the floor;
he made strange noises; he sneezed out-
rageously. Altogether he was a most uncom-
fortable travelling companion. The climax was
reached, however, when he pulled out an
abominable pipe and began stuffing it with
black twist. His companion nudged him,

whispered a few Gaelic words, and looked towards us. Then he spoke for him in a gentle drawl : " Would it disturb the lady if Mick had a pull at the pipe ? " I was as angry with one as the other. I thought I was applied to because I happened to be the best-dressed woman in the carriage. I answered sharply, " No, he can't smoke. These ladies would object, and he has no right to smoke here." Mick was rather inclined to smoke without permission, but his companion finally dissuaded him.

At Chester I got out for a cup of tea, and felt morally certain that my Irish harvestmen would be removed before I came back by the strong arm of the law. I rather wonder that little girl didn't see to it before she collected her own traps. However, I dare say she was a selfish young monkey, and only resented infractions of the law when they seemed to affect herself. She had disappeared when I got back. Her place was taken by a heavily-veiled widow. The harvesters were still there.

They were at the far end of the carriage, which was obscure, that wet December day, and the hurrying porters had not noticed them. I was disgusted. I was half-tempted to invoke the law myself; only I was Irish, and so, with a rooted conviction that the law always takes the wrong side in a quarrel, I sat down gingerly in my seat opposite to them.

I had hardly sat down when the two stood up. They deposited their bundles, and proceeded to get out of the carriage. I saw they thought the train would not start for an indefinite period, and had been slowly making up their minds to get out. A warning was on my lips, when I drew back cruelly. They were a good riddance I thought. Conscience pricked me, but I answered it: " What does it matter ? At the worst they'll be sent on by the next train ? Why should they gall all these people, and so disgrace the old country ? Besides, they've no *right* here." With which pronouncement I sat firmly back in my corner. I saw the two Sisters look at each other with a deprecating question. No one spoke, however ; but as the two frieze-coated figures disappeared I think we all felt vaguely guilty. There were the two poor bundles staring us in the face ; and suddenly out of a mysterious brown paper parcel, which the elder man had tenderly deposited in the corner, came a little sweet twitter. There was a bird there, and with the knowledge I suddenly felt an overpowering sense of meanness. I stood up, and hurried to the door. A porter was slamming the doors of the carriages. The train began to move. Just then I saw the two men running. The elder was a good bit ahead. I beckoned to him frantically, somewhat to my own surprise. He gained on the slowly-moving train, and bounded in at the door I held open, just as the pace lengthened. My conscience was salved, even though I saw my other countryman in the grip of two porters, as he was essaying a desperate leap after his companion.

It made me feel doubly guilty when the poor fellow began to shower blessings on me in

mixed Gaelic and English. "Sure what would
he have done, with all the dures closed an' him
not knowin' where to turn, an' his little blind
colleen in Kilnaree expecting him to-morrow,
sure." I sat with the smug smile of the
hypocrite on my lips.

Presently he fell to bemoaning Mick. Mick
was all right, I assured him jauntily; he would
be despatched by next train. "And you will
be at home before him, so that his people won't
be anxious," I said. I wasn't really concerned
about Mick and his people—not to the extent
of inquiring who might be expecting Mick in
Kilnaree. Without that too-pronounced companion my friend began to show to advantage.
His English was not fluent. It did not seem
to rise easily to his lips. What he had was the
delightful Irish-English, with the Gaelic idioms
transplanted, making the sentences curiously
roundabout and discursive. The slowness of
speech consorted with the infinite patience of his
face. His voice was rich and sweet in its de-
liberate wail. As he went on talking I could see

that there was a reaction of public opinion, and that now it tended in his favour. He was as frank about his poor little affairs as the little girl had been two hours ago, but with a difference. His little colleen—" O, she was blind, from taking the measles when it was a baby, she was, and the mother of her being dead, the creature, there was no one to keep her from getting cold, and the measles they got into her eyes, and she was 'dark' ever since. It's for her the bird is, and 'tis herself will be glad when she hears him singing, for 'tis lonely for a dark child in Kilnaree, an' Mrs. Murphy, that she does live with, my own mother's cousin, 'tis an old woman she is, an' no companion for the *girsha*. But Mary Doyle, that's the priest's housekeeper, an' a good scholar, she writes her the weeny letters, an' so it's not as bad when I do be harvestin' in England as if no word come at all to say was she dead or alive. She fretted terrible when ould Pincher, that we had from a pup, died, so I'm bringin' her the bird, an' would your ladyship like to see it? It has a grand song entirely, an' it's Patrick's Day I'm trying to teach it, but it isn't good at learnin' tunes whatever, only the weeshy song it picks up itself."

He untied the string of the parcel and disclosed a fine green cage, in which a very tiny canary sat all in a chilly little bunch and looked at us inquiringly. He had evidently been kindly treated and knew his friends, for seeing the dark face leaning over him he broke into a glad little whistle. His master looked delighted at the ready recognition, and began to whistle "The Blackbird" very low and sweet. The canary burst into a merry trill of rivalry. So they whistled against each other, man and bird, till the canary's song became rather piercing. Then his master pulled down the brown paper curtain, and the bird retired to sleep, being under the impression it was night.

It was growing to late afternoon, indeed, by this time, and we were approaching Bangor. All the women in the carriage had leaned together over the happy *séance* of music. Our harvester was telling us how he bought the canary from a foreign man with earrings. "He had finches too, an' blackbirds, an' thrushes, an' lonely the creatures looked in their cages. The blackbird, that's cheerful at home wid us, an' lookin' well fed, whin the rest of us can't keep the life in us, sure it's desolate he was an' mopin'. Now, Dick, here, he's used to the cage, and would be fair lost out in the wide world. I told the fellow some ould *pishrogue* about the unluckiness it was to take the wild birds, but he shook his ringlets an' his earrings, as though he didn't understand. I bought Dick, an' it's the comfort he has been to me, many a time when I'd have been sorrowful widout him."

I asked him weren't the Welsh hills like Ireland. They were looming one after the other out of the rain, and a bit of stormy sunset in the west was turning their wet flanks to vivid rose-colour. "Like the part you come from, me lady," he said, "but wid us at Kilnaree there's no more risin' than dawny little sand-

hills, though I'm thinkin' wid the stones on the
fields you might build mountains as big as
them out there."

We had by this time got to Bangor. I
thought he had quite forgotten Mick in our
pleasant conversation, but I found he hadn't.
He got up when the train slackened. "How
long here, yer ladyship?" he asked. "Five
minutes," I replied. "Then I'm thinkin' I'll
go spake to the station-master about Mick. It's
the first time the boy was in England, an' it's
lost he'll be entirely, besides having little of the
English." I didn't dissuade him, and he got
out with a cheerful warning from his erstwhile
reluctant companions to hurry back. But, alas!
the poor fellow had barely plunged towards the
booking office when the train was off. I suppose
I had made a mistake about the time, or he had
been slow in getting out. I saw his despairing
look and rush towards the train, but he was too
late. We were flying on toward the Menai
Bridge, and he had shared Mick's fate of being
left behind.

I suppose our consternation would only be possible to a crowd of women. The misfortune that had seemed so remediable in Mick's case was hopeless in this. It seemed to us all, somehow, as if our guilty acquiescence at Chester had entailed this misfortune. There were the two forlorn bundles, knotted in red-spotted cotton handkerchiefs, and each hung to a stick, staring at us. But the bird was the last touch of the pathos of the situation. We uncovered the cage to see if he was well-provisioned. It was as clean as possible, and seed-drawers and water-pot were full. Poor Dick opened his eyes drowsily at the sudden influx of daylight, and, seeing only strangers, began to fly up and down in terror and bewilderment. I've never thought of Dick since without a pang. We did the best possible. At Holyhead I selected the gentlest-faced porter I could see, and gave the lost canary into his hands, with explicit instructions how to identify its master. I telegraphed back to the station-master at Bangor :—" Let Irish harvestman left behind know his canary awaits him here." Then I went aboard the boat, feeling that I was a miserable creature in spite of my joy ahead. I wonder were the canary and his master reunited? I wonder how the little "dark" child at Kilnarec took her disappointment of December 22? I have no means of knowing. I trust all came right, and for Mick too; that the Fates were less intolerant to them than one born like those two "kindly Irish of the Irish."

SHAMEEN.*

"AH, musha, Larry," said the man on the other side of the long car to our driver, "did you hear that James Hurley was dead? The news came to Miss Dempsey at the post office from her brother at Cincinnati."

Our carman pulled up so suddenly that it would have twisted the mare's mouth if she had not been very leisurely ascending the sweet mountain road. As it was, she only shook herself with a mute remonstrance, and went on more leisurely.

"Ah, thin, Shameen!" said the carman, with the most wonderful tenderness, "ah, thin, is Shameen dead? God rest you, Shameen!

* Anglicè, "little James." The diminutive "een" is constantly applied in Ireland as a term of affection.

Sure it was you could lighten the road for the mare with the lilt of a song."

Rosa and I looked at each other. It sounded the sweetest lamentation in the crooning Irish voice. The driver of the long car was a great ruddy fellow, square-faced, dark-haired, determined-looking, as one often sees them in that country where Noll's troopers intermarried with violet-eyed daughters of the mere Irish. An excellent fellow was Larry Hayes, and we had made several trips with him ; for his long car which conveyed the mails and a stray traveller or two passed through an enchanting stretch of country. He had quite a friendly interest in us and our excursions. We had got brown and cheerful in our month that was now well-nigh ended. To-day there was a dull silver of rain in the air from morning. Last night there were gusts that carpeted the valley with scarlet and orange, and the woods that had been gloriously clothed showed only ragged banners of colour like the fragments of glory one sees hanging high in the cathedral at home.

The rainy day broke up splendidly. It had been almost too dark in the early afternoon for Rosa to sketch those ruins we tramped to in the mild mist. Now the western heaven opened, and we saw the passage, as it were, of a myriad angels, flying on in steady, long flight, golden-headed, golden-gowned, golden-feathered; with now and then a glimpse of delicate rose, as though one caught sight of a young cheek or a naked foot in the rifts of gold.

The other passenger on the long car we had picked up as he trudged steadily along on his way home from a distant fair. He communicated all his news of "Shameen" stolidly; how he had died in hospital, and how Miss Dempsey's brother had heard of it from a priest, and how his death had been the result of an accident on the railway where he was employed, in which it seemed he had given his life to rescue some worthless one.

We listened for a while, and at last one of us said, "Who was Shameen, Larry?"

G

"Is it Shameen Hurley, Miss? Well, thin, I'll tell you," was the reply; "an' it's not to every one I'd talk about Shameen this day. You know Knockmeelderry over there? It's the handsome hill, an' it's the first to see the sun in the mornin' an' the last to bid him good-bye at night. Well, Shameen's little house an' farm was under the big flank of Knockmeelderry; an' indeed there was a time he was like what I'm after tellin' you of that same hill, for he was always lookin' at the sun—an' such a voice—he'd coax the birds off the trees with it. Eh, ladies, it's the quare world it is intirely. He was the manliest fellow in the three parishes. He was big an' gentle an' good. Good! he was as good as a pot of goold. He lived all alone, did Shameen, with just an old woman to come in an' clear up for him. The girls used to be sayin' it was a quare way for him to be, an' how much more he'd get out o' the farm if he'd a wife to see after the butter an' the calves an' the pigs for him. They

wor all leppin' to get him, but, indeed, though
he'd always the soft word for a woman or a
child, aye, and for a dumb baste, he gev no
girl raison to suppose he was thinkin' of her.
The boy was too innocent to know how they
wor all round him like flies around honey.
His father was handsome an' bad. There
wasn't a bit of badness in all Shameen's body.
He was his mother's son, and she was the
best an' sweetest girl in the barony, an' when
she found out the man she was married to, the
crathure, she died of it. They said it was
consumption she died of, my brown little
girl; but it wasn't, it was *silent contimpt.*
When she found out what he was, an' she
had adored him, the love went back on her
heart an' killed her."

Larry's thoughts were evidently far back
in the past, and we had a clue to them, for
we had heard how "an ould, ancient love-
affair" had made him the determined bachelor
he was.

"Shameen was like his mother," he went

on dreamily; "he took things hard. I was terrible fond of him from a boy. He was always bright an' glad to gladden my heart, till he fell in love; an' as misfortunes never come alone, no sooner was he in it over head an' ears than th' ould Captain that was kind went an' died on us, an' the naygur that's there now," shaking his whip at a distant turret, "fell in for the place. Eh, but she was purty, little Susy O'Brien; an' her father, ould Kendal, the richest and closest-fisted farmer in the county. I often wonder if Shameen had known the misfortunes that was comin' to him, whether he wouldn't have kep' out of her way, but I don't know. It was like as if it was to happen, an' he was like his mother—love was hell or heaven to him; he was like her in another way, too, for he was terrible proud.

"They said Susy came home from the Convent wantin' to be a nun, an' that ould Kendal was mad about it. I misdoubted that story from the first day I seen her in the chapel;

for though she was as demure-lookin' as a statue, she had a pair of funny little dimples that crep' about in her cheeks, an' as we were comin' out I saw her givin' a long look at some one from under her eyelashes, an' whin I looked it was Shameen, an' faith he was starin' at her as if he'd ate her. Purty she was; she was like a little wisp of thistledown, so light an' airy she was, an' her face was as innocent as a daisy, and soft an' pale, an' set in hair like fine goold. She was delicate-lookin', an' yet wholesome-lookin'.

"Ladies, did yez ever hear of a love that sprung up an' took root an' got strong in two hearts without ever a word of love being spoken? Well, that was the way with Susy an' my poor Shameen. They met at neighbours' houses, at weddin's and dances, at the chapel on Sunday, and Shameen seemed drawn wherever she was, an' yet determined to keep away from her. But he couldn't help *lookin'*, an' as time went on, though nobody suspected but me, yet I saw their looks once or twice, and wondered the world didn't know. The colleen would look at him appealin' as if she thought he was angry, an' he'd look back at her with his face cold an' pale, but his eyes full of fire. I've heard of the love-light; but poor Shameen's love-light was more like a consumin' fire. He got haggard and quare, an' even his sweet songs he changed for ould lamentations an' the like; that is whenever you'd get him to sing, for it was seldom. On his little place things was goin' from bad to worse with him. I consoled myself thinkin' that ould Kendal for all his nearness wouldn't deny his one little girl the wish of her heart, seein' that Shameen was so likely a lad, an' his misfortunes not of his own makin'.

"Eh, I'd reckoned without Shameen's pride. Shameen beggared would never ask for a rich man's daughter. It was seven years ago last May, Clonmel fair-day. For a wonder I'd no passengers, an' I was just lettin' the mare take her time. I was heavy in heart, for I knew things wor in a bad way with Shameen. He'd gone to Dublin to see the agent an' ask for time. Well, quite suddenly a man jumped up out o' the ditch where he'd been lyin' on his face. Glory be to God it was Shameen, yet none need have blamed me if I hadn't known him at first. His dress was tossed and disordhered as if he'd been lyin' out all night. He looked as wake an' quare as if food hadn't seen the inside of him for a fortnight ; his hair was tossed an' wild : but it was none of them things made the terrible change in Shameen ; it was the dead sick look of misery in his eyes. Before I could spake to him he spoke to me, in a quare, cracked voice. 'Don't talk to me, Larry,' he said, ' I'm goin' to take a sate with you as far as the Junction ; I'm off to America.' 'Off to America,' says he, as aisy as if he was talkin' of Emly or Golden. Well, the poor lad, I troubled him but little, but as we went on he told me he was out of his farm—that visit to the agent had only quickened things for him.

"We went along an' along, and the sweet

May evenin' it was, an' the blackbird—that
used always to stop when Shameen began—
singin' fit to crack his throat, and all the
pleasant country so quiet, by raison of the
people bein' in the chapel attendin' to their
May devotions. I was sick to say somethin'
to him of Susy, but faith I didn't like to ; he
was leanin' down like an ould bent man, an'
more betoken, fond as he was of me, I'd found
out that Shameen could be very proud an' cold
over his saycrets.

"How did she find out at all, at all ? Or
what instinct brought her there ?—Och, sure,
women are wonders when they're in love. It
was in the loneliest part o' the road that she
suddenly stepped out of a *boreen* where she
was standin'. She ran up like a child with her
hands out, and I could see all her purty face
pinched like a snow-drop that's caught in the
frost. My poor Shameen gev a big cry, and
then jumped off—and the mare an' myself had
the sense just to move on a bit and let the
crathures have their say to themselves. An' I,

the big fool I was,—was all in a pucker of
delight, thinkin' I needn't drive Shameen to
the Junction after all. Och, *wirra, wirrasthrue,*
it's a quare world, an' it's only when you're
ould an' lonely and the pain over that you
begin to see what value love was, and how
little the gabbin' tongues o' people matthered,
so long as you had the love.

"It was only a minit anyhow.   He hadn't
more nor time to kiss her purty lips once or
twice when he was back. 'Drive on,' he says, in
a terrible, hard, dry voice that gives me an ache
to think of even now.   I said no more till the
train was steamin' an' him in it.   I was ould
enough to be his father, an' might have been
that same, but I couldn't question him : I
hadn't courage.   Lookin' at his face, though, I
tried, wettin' my lips with my tongue, for they
were both dry with anxiety.   He squeezed up
in the corner of the carriage, an' looked straight
before him in a dead sort of way.   I stood with
my hand on the window, but I'm misdoubting
he knew a friend was there at all, at all.   'Did

you spake to the little girl, Shameen?' I said at last; 'she's the thrue little girl that'd wait for you.' 'No,' said he, lookin' at me straight, 'why should I spake to a rich man's daughter?' 'Well, thin, God forgive you, Shameen,' said I; but sure in the middle of it the whistle came, and that was my last word with Shameen.

.   .   .   .   .

"An' little Susy, Miss? Well, she drooped, an' then she took up a bit, like as if she was hopeful. The father tried to make her match half-a-dozen times, but she gev them all the go-by. But, sure, you can't live on hope for ever, an' as the months went an' no tale or tidin's of Shameen, she grew slindherer, an' quieter. Miss Dempsey told me afterwards that she gev up by degrees callin' for the post; an' the little screeds from the nuns an' the school friends were called for by Thady Murphy, the boy from the forge. I seen her once lookin' like a little red rose: that was a few months after Shameen left, an' I'm thinkin' it was the thought of his kiss an' his arms about her brought the purty colour in her cheeks. Ochone, the blight came on as it might on the same little red rose. Less than two years after Shameen went, they buried her. I wonder whether he ever heard. Anyhow, from that day to this no word of mouth or letter came from him. But, sure, he's spoken the word now. God is good; an' I'll go bail the love that never was spoken between them on earth was tould out full an' free when she ran to meet him, the darlin', over the pavemints of Heaven."

We were creeping up the hill to the town by this time. We were all silent, in sympathy with Larry's emotion; he only spoke once afterwards, and then it was to the mare,—

"Sheila, my honey, do you remember Shameen? Ah! poor Shameen's dead! An', sure, it was many a long an' hard road he lightened for you with the lilt of a song. He made your heart bate so light you never felt the load. But he's done singin' on earth long ago, Sheila!"

A MARTYR INDEED.

THE house is in the midst of a wide tract of fields. The only approach is by a stony *boreen* from the cheerful high road, where the mountain farmers are going home of an evening, and the scattered cottages show children under a thatch of sun-bleached hair, and dogs are barking, and ducks are quacking in procession as they paddle along the running waterways by the path. It is within reach of the shrill whistle of the steam-tram. Yet so lonely, so unspeakably solitary. There is no such loneliness as that of the evening fields, more especially if it be Autumn. Wandering in the vicinity of the house one September evening, a-mushroom-gathering, I remember to have lost for a little while my companion. He was

only in the shadow of the distant hedge, amid
the fairy rings on the grass, where one finds
the mushrooms cleverly covered up in the rich
growth of those mysterious circles. Yellow
was all the sky above the mountains. The
evening had grown cold. I looked through
the thorn hedges on top of a little bank, and
saw across the narrow field the fireless chimneys
of the old house. It looked quite dead. I
shivered with a sudden sense of desolation and
fear. The loneliness did not affect me as it
did a nervous small boy who lived in just such
fields, with only an elder and morose brother
for society. "When a hen croaks," he said to
me, "I feel as if I must scream. And then I
want to wring the damned thing's neck." I
stole away from the vicinity of the house as
though invisible ears might hear my tread on
the grass, and got back as speedily as possible
to my kind.

Yet quite within my memory the place had
been comfortable and homely enough. That was
before the Laverys, mother and daughter, went

down hill at the pace that brought them to the
bottom within a very short time. The father was
dead then, happily for himself. He had held
his head high, poor man, and was even wealthy;
the money he put into the building of our
beautiful church ran into three figures. When
I knew the daughter, who was the evil influence
of her family, she was elderly, and hideous
with affectation and a certain brazen hardness that was natural to her. I remember
the drawing-room in the taste of the day.
Glaring satin paper of a dead white; gilt
mouldings round the cornices; a big chan-
delier with many diamond drops glittering
from it; and what was called a *suite* of
furniture, in grass-green rep, completed the
finethings.

We were hunted, we youngsters, out to the
garden to eat gooseberries. There were strawberries too under the high wall that makes a black
shadow with its masses of ivy. The currants
swung like jewels there in that plenty one only
sees in an ancient garden. All around stood

up the big trees, silent sentinels of the place.
And away at the far end of the garden the
little house, gray and green, and covered with
jessamine and monthly roses, might have made
a paradise for some one.

We were not deceived, we youngsters, while
we devoured the ripe fruit. With all the acuteness
of small demoiselles we detected and giggled
over the absurdities of our hostess, her mincing
airs, her absurd pronunciation, her dress-im-
prover and high-heeled boots. We had not dared
to laugh before her, though the laughter was
importunate ; all the world knows the helpless
tittering to which school-girls are subject, and
which takes them at the most awful moments.
But though a drawing-room recitation drove us
behind the window curtains to lie strangling
with our laughter on the floor, we did not
dare laugh before our hostess that afternoon.
Through all her *minauderies* her hard eyes
kept their stare,—steely I should call it, if it
were not that their colour was a curious reddish-
brown—and it had scant toleration for us, even

when we kept our countenances with intense composure.

The old mother sat in a chair and grumbled and mumbled to herself in a half imbecile fashion. The brother came into the room once, as if by accident,—a square-jawed melancholy man, with colourless skin, and a down-drawn sad mouth ; he had a timid air that belied his square jaw, and when he shuffled away awkwardly we were inclined to think him a poor creature. However, later on, strolling around the house impudently, we came on him having his tea in the kitchen. We were inclined to run away in wild shrieks of laughter; but he came out to us with an air of awkward kindness. I rather think the parlour tea was over, and we, little pitchers, perhaps designedly, forgotten. The two elder visitors were able to discuss bonnets and beaux ; and we were supposed to be kept out of mischief fruit-eating in the garden.

He invited us to join him at his tea, which invitation was supplemented by a white-capped ruddy-faced old woman he called Biddy. " Come in, come in, little ladies," she said. " It isn't often the master has company to his tay." There was something at once defiant of some person or persons unknown, and yet kindly, in the tone of this invitation. We came in somewhat timidly. He helped her to set the chairs, and suggested this or that dainty : a pot of honey it was one time, the currant cake another. He seemed to like our company, though his melancholy face only brightened for a minute when, getting confident, we told him of our naughtiest escapades. The kitchen was clean and comfortable despite its clay floors, and the black thatch of the roof coming through the rafters. A wood-fire smouldered cheerfully, and there were geraniums in the high window. A screen of wall projected by the side of the fireplace ; and before the embers basked a collie and three kittens, in close friendship.

The master of the house did the honours of his deal table with great courtesy. We noticed

H

that as Biddy went here and there, polishing a plate or lifting the hot griddle-cakes from the fire, she turned always that steady look of affection on her master's face. It was as evident as the love in the eyes of the collie. We chattered while we ate and drank, and altogether enjoyed ourselves highly. When Biddy was summoned by the parlour-bell to go in search of us, she dismissed us each with a hot griddle-cake and a compliment. She pronounced us "rale dacint little ladies," and went on, half to herself: "I haven't seen the master so cheered for a long time." And then to us: "Yez'll be welcome whenever yez come, an' most av' the week herself is gallivantin' to Dublin, so yez can ate all yez can of the strawberries while they last." The master, too, shook hands with us when we went out to the primitive yard, where he was standing gazing at his manure heap and two ducks cocking inquiring eyes at the steady promise of fine weather in the sky. He even volunteered to show us the pups the next time we came, which we promised should be soon, and so we rejoined our elders and departed.

We never went again. By the time we came back from school the following year things had gone to the bad with them, and we knew them and the place no more.

I pieced the story afterwards from what was told me. There were of the family two sons and the daughter. The father was a man of ambitions ; the mother, as occasionally happens, of no ambitions at all, liking, if her husband's back was turned, nothing so well as a long confidential chat with the servants or the farm-hands. This mark of favour they repaid by summing up Mrs. Lavery as "a rale mane sort, wid a low drop in her somewhere." Adding, "God help poor Jimmy Lavery if he ever thinks to make a lady of *her !*" For the Irish peasant, though you can be extremely friendly with him or her, knows just where an equal familiarity begins, and is apt much to despise folk who cannot keep their places.

The girl was the apple of old Jimmy's eye.

The elder son he educated so well that the young gentleman became an army doctor, and, meeting and marrying the plain heiress of a Lancashire manufacturer, drifted away, happily for himself, from his doomed family. Michael, the younger, was always dull and gentle. He too went to the expensive school selected for his brother; but such ill reports of his wits came home, that, after a year or so, his father withdrew him, opining that there was no use in throwing good money after bad. Michael immediately began to forget the little polish and school learning he had acquired, and having a low opinion of himself he was happy, with no sense of injustice, plodding after the plough-horses or feeding the stall-feds; while old Jimmy, as his neighbours expressed it, "was swellin' like a bantam over his larned son and handsome daughter."

I have been told she was extremely hand-some as a girl. She was tall and straight, with a shape strong and supple. She had the beautiful complexion that goes with reddish hair sometimes. Her hair, which in my memory was in faded hanks of dull red, has been described to me as of great splendour of colour and abundance.

The country shook its head over Jimmy's fondness for his daughter. He sent her to boarding-school, and while she was away built a front for the house, which up to that had been entered by the kitchen. When it was finished he planted a little lawn with a carriage-drive; and malicious enemies had it that, in addition to "the pianny," this infatuated father had laid in "crokay for the quality to play at wid Miss 'Tilda." But when she came home "finished," his doings exceeded the wildest invention. The first thing he did was to set her up with a pony and phaeton; the next to equip her with a horse to ride to hounds.

This latter, among the conservative Irish peasants, made a positive scandal; and it was as bad with the neighbouring farmers, themselves but superior peasants. Not that any one could deny that on horseback she was twice as handsome as the Miss Bartons, and twice as haughty too. But, indeed, the Miss Bartons were soft-spoken young ladies, with no more beauty than clear skin and silky hair affords, and no more approach to haughtiness than the somewhat mild wonder with which they regarded this interloper in the hunting field; who soon, however, came to have plenty of acquaintances among the sons of the county families and the officers from the barracks.

When at home, this darling of her father sat and strummed wrong notes on the piano in the fine white-and-gold drawing-room he had provided for her; or stared listlessly into the fire or out of the window, if she was alone: but often she had a school-friend to visit her, one who would listen to her conquests and admire her beauty, for none other would be tolerated. Occasionally, too, a gentleman came to call. Even sprigs of nobility were entertained in that chilly apartment. But when his girl was at the height

of her social success,—for Jimmy, poor man,
had not yet found out that the acquaintance
of fine gentlemen is not the mark of ladyhood—fortunately, for himself, he took suddenly ill and died.

To 'Tilda, no doubt, it seemed all right that
Michael should plod along in the old patient
way, with no more consideration now that he
was master. The mother, who grew more
whining and down-at-heel year by year, father
and daughter had long agreed to ignore.
Michael would have fared badly if it were not
for Biddy who had nursed him, and loved him
with a protecting fondness that was in proportion to the hostility she had always entertained
towards his sister. 'Tilda would have been
contemptuously amused if she had known ; but
then, she never thought of a servant, except
as Biddy put it, "like dirt under her feet ; "
and she probably considered the old servant
constitutionally sullen.

She was hard and masculine enough to
have taken care of herself, even then. I have

heard how she rubbed her horse down, and washed her phaeton herself, when she found it quite impossible to get those things satisfactorily done by a farm hand. But I imagine she was a creature without moral stamina. Anyhow, in the very heyday of her beauty some mysterious scandal arose about her. I know nothing of the story or its origin : it is all so long ago : but it stuck to her, and manifested itself so unpleasantly in the hunting-field, that after a time she sold her mare, and went riding no more.

Michael heard it in time. It put wrinkles in his face and gray hairs on his head. He began to grow into a patient drudge, without youth or hope. Yet he kept the place going somehow, and things were scarcely less prosperous in a monetary sense than of old.

The scandal had almost blown over when his first and only bit of romance came to him. What Nellie Curran, the tall, gipsy beauty saw in him, Heaven knows ! Nellie's father, too, was one of the snuggest men in the

county, and she the only chick or child
he had. Her mother was Nellie's predecessor
in goodness and beauty. She was the finest
housekeeper for miles round ; and her goodness included everything under its wide wings.
It was she who first began the rehabilitation
of 'Tilda Lavery. It was by dropping a
kind word here or there. " Well, Mrs.
Burke," she would say, " I do be thinking
there was nothing in that story at all, at all.
Sure none could tell where the weeny whisper
came from that blackened the creature. God
help us, sure the devil is powerful when he
goes scandal-mongering. Anyhow, you and
me has *girleens* of our own, and for their
sakes it's not every story against poor 'Tilda
I'd go to be believing." Gradually a kind of
feeling got about that 'Tilda Lavery had been
condemned on insufficient evidence. In con-
trition for having been so ready to believe
ill of the child of an old neighbour, people
began to make advances to her. She accepted
the civilities, and was seen at one or two

houses ; but, despite the good intentions of the contrite, people didn't seem to take to her. Nor did she seem very anxious to be sociable. Save for those drives in the phaeton, which she still kept up, she was seen little outside her own isolated home.

Meanwhile Nellie Curran had cast glances of pitying tenderness on Michael Lavery. He used to pass the Currans' comfortable farmhouse now and again by a field-path that was a short cut to another road. He went by at first with his head down in his habitual attitude of dejection. Miss Nellie met him one evening, blooming in her pink frock, with starry eyes and cheeks like a ripe peach. She was a young lady to take her affairs into her own hands. She conquered Michael Lavery very easily. From the first the poor fellow was but full of awe-struck wonder that this young goddess should be civil to him. All one happy summer his idyll lasted. He wasn't wanted at home, and used to spend the long evenings, when the ruddy light took hours to grow cool in the sky, hanging in a moon-struck way about the Currans' house. There was no doubt that Nellie was fond of him. She bloomed like a Camille de Rohan rose ; and she was so kind to her lover, never teasing him, but treating him rather with a placid motherly tenderness that was very sweet. Her father opined humorously that Nellie was picking up the crooked stick—for her rejections had reached a respectable number; her mother sighed when Nellie was not by. She had hoped for better things for her lovely daughter, though no one could deny that a better poor lad than Michael Lavery never existed, and well off too. Anyhow, if he had been much less eligible, Nellie was bound to have her way.

Half the country was wondering why he didn't speak, when the thing happened that closed his lips for ever. He came home from Nellie one night, under an enormous August moon, half beside himself with happiness. The hall-door was wide open as he approached.

Instead of going to the kitchen, he went in
that way, and turned the handle of the parlour
door on his left. There was no light in the
room, but it perfectly reeked with the fumes of
brandy. He struck a match and looked about
him. His mother was lying back in her chair,
her cap disordered, her head lolling in the
stertorous sleep of the drunkard. His sister
was on the floor in the same condition ; some
one had thrust a pillow under her head. The
match flickered out in his fingers, as he
stumbled to the door. In the kitchen was old
Biddy, her apron over her head, while she
rocked to and fro. " How long has this been
going on ? " he said, with dry lips. " This
many a month," the old woman moaned out,
" but I was always able to get them out of the
way before you kem home. O *wirrasthrue*,"
she went on, " don't be lookin' like that,
darlin'! Sure I thought you'd be married, an'
wid the darlin' wife of your own before you
knew the black shame and disgrace."

He turned from her and went up to his attic.

Many evenings after that, pretty Nellie looked
for her lover, but he never came. She kept
up her heart till the Sunday morning, when she
was sure to see him at mass. He was not
there, having gone at daybreak to a distant
parish. Then Nellie was determined to see
for herself. She set out for the house in the
fields, hoping fortune would favour her. Nellie
didn't much like 'Tilda; and as she explained
it herself, old Mrs. Lavery "gave her the
creeps." But she walked as close to the house
as she could—perhaps by that very hedge
where I peeped through to see the silent house.
She came upon him suddenly, leaning on a
gate in a forlorn attitude. She went up to him
confidently, sure of her beauty and his love;
but when he saw her, a scared look came into
his eyes, and lifting his hat hastily, he turned
away and went back to the house.

Nellie walked home with her heart bursting.
She refused obstinately at first to believe him
guilty of ill-treating her. She even wrote to
him, and received in reply a dull missive that

betrayed nothing of his heart-break. Presently, being a girl of spirit, she plucked up; she made herself angry to kill out that dull pain of rejected tenderness that was in her heart. The anger made her handsomer than ever; her proud step, her haughty head, her lovely colour, flashed themselves into the gallant heart of a hunting *squireen* from a neighbouring county. Six months after she had been jilted by Michael Lavery—she said it over to herself till it grew meaningless, in order to keep up her spirit—she married her *squireen*, and is to this day the delight of her husband's eyes.

That all happened ten years before that visit of ours to the Laverys. How the poor fellow kept the scandal quiet, God knows. Biddy helped him; and he turned off the labourers by degrees, so that the house was left more lonely. The farm went rather to the bad. After a time he parted with some of the fields, and pastured a few depressed-looking beasts on the remainder. Those ten years

had made him prematurely middle-aged. His
mother was half imbecile. His sister as I have
described her, with nothing of her old beauty
but her height. Her brother she despised and
hated. He let her go where she would and
do what she would, but he did his best to keep
her from smuggling her brandy into the house,
so that the wretched old mother should not get
it. 'Tilda Lavery had a constitution and
nerves of iron. Her potations seemed to
have had little effect on her health when I saw
her. However the whole thing came out in
the following year. What I heard of the
exposure is too painful, and the story is only
worth telling because of poor Michael Lavery's
unconscious heroism. During that year the
mother ended her dishonoured life, after a
horrible three months, when the shame had
been blazoned abroad, and the house in the
fields was left to its wintry darkness, and the
daughter rioted unrestrainedly while the mother
lay dying. It was a relief when she was dead.
The funeral was attended by all the old neigh-

bours, many of whom longed to say a kind word to the poor fellow who had suffered so much. They said he looked a gaunt figure of despair by the graveside. He returned to the lonely house where only poor affectionate Biddy awaited him. 'Tilda was gone as soon as the breath was out of her mother's body ; and the most dreadful stories were afloat about her. However, I never knew any one who saw her again or heard of her decisively.

.   .   .   .   .

Michael Lavery never goes to his parish church now, nor to fair or market, where he might meet his fellow-men. He has got into the habit of avoiding them, but I have met him once or twice on my evening walks, and he looks kindly despite his great melancholy. I saw him on Wednesday, that wonderful evening of rosy sunset. The mountains were pink and blue, blent like the colours of a forget-me-not. The trees in the lane showed a delicate brown outline against the roses. Long after, below the coppery-brown night that was swallowing the West, the rosy light peeped forth, and its reflection tinged in the East many rosy bodies of clouds floating on the filmy azure. Michael Lavery struck a dreary note in the lovely world. His face is gray and lean between its sparse side whiskers. He walks with stooped shoulders like one long used to carrying a burden. He is unkempt, dusty, forlorn, solitary. Biddy is dead; and the white and gold drawing-room, I have heard, is a store-house for potatoes. There is not even a dog attached to the place. Michael Lavery and the rats are alone. For twelve years now he has lived alone; he will die alone. The house has grown half-ruined, and the windows are broken. It had such a bad name that the village urchins delighted to fling stones at the windows when the solitary master was out of hearing in the kitchen where he lives. That Wednesday night was wild, and I thought that some such night might bring it tumbling about his ears. If he were gone it were well the house, with all its bad memories, were gone too, and the grass growing where once its desecrated hearthstone lightened. There is a vague pity for Michael Lavery; but few of the neighbours have reached the point of calling him, as I do, a martyr. Perhaps it would seem profane to those simple minds.

A FARMER'S TRAGEDY.

IT is a year since I met that mournful procession going home by green lanes. The
blackbirds sang in mad rivalry just the
same ; croak, croak went the corn-crake, the
harsh voice of the summer ; the meadows were
turning brown, yellow iris was springing on her
green flaggers ; the hawthorn, as now, was
turning to pink, making every bush look a more
lavish bower of little roses than Botticelli's
Spring herself could furnish forth.

Such a divine, dewy, green evening, with the
fragrance of a censer in the air ; and there was
coming towards me in the narrow lane a line of
labourers marching dejected, a horse and cart
following. I could not avoid it if I would. I
had spoken to the man at the horse's head
before I saw the thing that answered my

question—something lying stark and awful, under the sacks in the cart, that dimly outlined a human shape, with the rigid dead feet pointing upwards. There was no need to ask who it was. The farmer's son had been missing for some weeks, and I had heard of his loss with a vague curiosity, which now quickened into appalled interest. He had been lying all those weeks in a pool, the waters of which scarcely covered him. No one had thought of searching the place, though every quarry-hole and pond had been dragged. It was in a lonely field, turning to a meadow, in the midst of which is a curious *dun* or fort on a mound. They say that somewhere below it, choked up, led a subterranean passage to a great old house of the neighbourhood. He must have drowned himself, poor lad, with the terrible determination of the insane; must have lain face downward in the mud of the place where they found him; lain all those weeks in sunrise and sunset, while the larks had soared out of the grass beside him, and the little cottage-children had

filed by the hedge not many yards away, looking for birds' nests and eggs speckled and blue.

The only son of his father ; but his mother's
son, one felt sure.   He had nothing in common
with the dour, hard-faced, hard-fisted old man,
whom age had no power to break or soften.
His mother died the merest slip of a girl.
She had, I have heard, this boy's silky pale
hair and clear skin, and large frightened eyes.
They had married her with as much sentiment
as one sells a heifer at the market.   Her old
husband—for he was old even then—was the
richest man of the country-side, and the aunt
and uncle who had the giving of her considered
her a right lucky girl.   They took her out of
her convent school and her gentle, merry girl-
hood, and gave her over to this grey husband.
I have heard he was very gentle with her, but
in the months they were married she grew a
wofully frightened creature, shrinking from him,
the people said, and incessantly weeping when
she could steal away by herself.   So it was no
wonder that when this boy was born she had

not the vitality to pull through. If she had
seen his face, indeed, she might have tried to
live for him—the acres and the dairy and the
jaunting-car, and the best parlour with roses on
the wall-paper, having proved all insufficient.
But she never rallied after the child was born,
just sinking into a stupor, which lasted till her
death a few hours later.

The old man asked no comfort, and would
take none. His face, they said, grew more
like a grey rock than ever, his hair went white
in quite a short time, but his sufferings—if
suffer he did—he bore with the proud stoicism
of an Indian brave. The child he never
noticed—seemed neither to love nor hate it.
But while the boy was young the soft-hearted
peasant-mothers made up for this coldness.
Katty, the old woman who was housekeeper
and general servant at the farm, adored him;
and when he was old enough to be led by the
hand as she went on this or that short errand,
the neighbour women overwhelmed him with
fondness and praise. Pity it could not last

always, this quiet childhood. But a time came when his father began to notice him as the heir to his land and his bank-notes. The old man should indeed have been the founder of a family. With incredible industry, and wonderful sagacity as well, he had added acre to acre and shilling to shilling, until he was actually extremely wealthy. And how he loved his land! It is the richest and kindliest land, with manure and drainage and labour buried in it like gold-dust, which it yields every year in smiling harvests. He gave it the love which had been thrown back on his heart by the wife who had cheated him of her love. I think he was no stony-hearted tyrant in the matter of the marriage. In his own youth he had never had time for love ; marriages were arranged so all about him : and the girl had been too timid to show her aversion so openly that he could read it. Then he loved her no doubt, and had recognized that marriage with him had killed her. Perhaps in this whimpering, pale-faced son he saw her aversion come to life again.

In a way it was hard upon him. Close-fisted
as he was, he had a certain largeness of view.
I think had his only son been but a fellow of
will and courage and ambition, the old father
would have opened his purse-strings and
lavished upon him the things that should give
a fair bent to his qualities. But *this* for his
only son ! This puling boy, who dissolved in
tears if he but looked at him, who dared
not sleep by himself for fear of hobgoblins,
who mooned incessantly with a dog at his heels,
and believed implicitly every superstition of the
peasantry. It turned him sick with anger to
think upon him. As he grew up it was no
better. He no longer wept, but he slunk out
of his father's way like a dog that has been
beaten once and may be again ; he crouched by
the hob if it was cold or wet ; he was always
being coddled by Katty for a chill or an ache ;
and in summer he desired no more than to be
hidden all day in the overgrown orchard at the
foot of the hill, reading a ragged book or a sheaf
of ballads purchased from the pedlar, or lying

in the grass with hands clasped below his head, gazing into the apple-boughs, where presently the horned moon should swing, and the screech-owl call her melancholy whistle.

He was very familiar with birds, and beasts, and plants ; very simple, devout, and imaginative.   A delicate lad, with easily jangled nerves and too large organs of belief and veneration, and with a capacity for a great affectionateness. What schooling he got was from a poor tutor, a disqualified candidate for the priesthood, who came to the house for a couple of years.   The old man despised his son too heartily to put him in competition with other boys at a boys' school.

He was always a devout lad, but when his tutor, whom he had grown attached to, had left him, he became absorbed in his prayers and devotions.   His walks now generally led him towards the church ; and, mushroom-gathering on a July evening, I have come upon him chanting his Rosary aloud to himself.   He was getting towards manhood when his father unfortunately began to think it was time to break him into his own ways. The boy himself had got the idea of being a priest. He did not dare to speak of it to his father, but his one confidant, a mild old curate yet awaiting the promotion never to come, did it for him. The old man laughed in his pastor's face with fierce scorn, and bade him mind his own business so very emphatically that the old priest bowed himself out with a forlorn sense of outrage.

The boy was turned into farm-work, and began from then to drift into a melancholy madness. I have seen him the forlornest figure, awkwardly stumbling behind a plough, on a high upland, against a grey winter sky : I have caught a glimpse of him, moon-struck and melancholy, standing by a hedge, while the mowing-machine sang on its way and the chattering women mocked behind his back. His long fair hair, neglected, grew into his eyes that looked at one dully, with a film of suffering on them. No one noticed the growing madness because he was so silent and gentle. It

was only afterwards that Katty tore her hair
and beat her breast, recalling little signs and
tokens that she had never recognized for such
terrible omen.

. . . .

The poor drowned body was buried, and
things went on their dreary way at the farmhouse. At first one scarcely knew if the father
suffered ; but gradually he broke down, and once
the failure set in it went with wonderful rapidity,
as is often the case with old people who keep
their strength and vigour long. He soon was
only able to creep about his room with a pair of
sticks, and then, after a little while, could not
leave his bed. He did not die at the top,
certainly. To the last his head kept its clear-
ness. The man he had put in command could
tell strange stories of his searching questions.
The master's mind still supervised the place,
though his eye was off it, and he had always
inspired so great a fear that things went wonderfully well, considering that he lay like a log.
Before he died he opened his mouth to speak

in bitterness, in a half soliloquy, of the widowed cousin who had made a feckless love-match long ago, but who had four tall, brave, handsome sons to inherit the land, which he had left them, despite his bitterness, and though he had kept them off in a half-envious hatred during life. Of the dead boy, of the dead wife, he said nothing while conscious, but old Katty heard their names fall from his lips between the death-rattles. "Poor Jemmie: I didn't know, Mary!" he muttered, at if he were trying to extenuate his harshness to their boy.

It was Tommy Hogan told me what happened at daybreak, just when the old farmer died. Tommy is a nut-brown, wizened man, oracular, of a singular deliberateness of speech and belief in himself. He it was who told me how the crows begin to build on the 1st of March, except it be Sunday, in which case they postpone till Monday morning. From him I have full details of "a fairy blast" he had as a child; among ghosts and fairies he is quite at

home, and his knowledge of their ways not to
be disputed. This morning of the old man's
death he, with others, was milking my father's
cows beside the boundary hedge of his farm.
I can picture it, for I saw the dawn that morning—a luminous green dawn, widening and
throbbing up the east, casting where it fell a
ghostly green light, and leaving all else in
blackest shadow. The hawthorn, that was
thick this year as cotton-wool on a Christmas-
tree, was ghastly in the cold light; the hills
were still wrapped in shrouds of mist; some
tree in the hedgerow kept up a sharp tinkling
like a field of barley; a little shiver of wind
was creeping along the earth, moaning amid
the seeding grasses that trembled as it passed.
The first birds were peering out, with an
inquiring twitter. The cows were folded in a
corner by an old house built on a fairy rath,
and of which I could tell another story an' I
would. The men were milking, not saying
much, each with his head in the cow's side, and
the air full of a cheerful sound of the milk

spirting in the pails.   They all knew that the
life of the old man at the house yonder among
the trees was running out to its last sands. Suddenly there came a noise, strange and terrible,
like a thunderclap out of a thundercloud, as
Tommy described it to me, and a cloud swept
by them out of which bellowed a howling wind,
blood-curdling and horrible.   The men fell on
their faces in its path ; the cattle broke away
madly, and were afterwards found many fields
distant.   Then, as the noise died in distance,
all things were again sweet and peaceful.   It
was Tommy who—when the scare was over,
and in the warm, golden dawn—explained the
thing.   " It was ould Mick," he said, " ridin' in
that whirlwind.   He couldn't go widout biddin'
good-bye to the land his heart was in.   He was
ridin' the boundaries of all his farm before lavin'
this world."   Sure enough it was just at the
hour old Mick Crowley drew his last breath.
And henceforth to the men who had shared with
him this terrifying experience, Tommy will be
more than ever a seer and an oracle.

FAREWELL TO BALLYSHANNON.

IT was as we were leaving the hotel door we first saw Johnny, and had a hint of the long journey he was bound on. All the morning there had been unwonted bustle in the big gray caravanserai, where men are for ever coming and going. We had heard many instructions called in a shrill, sweet voice; there was frequent passing of feet up and down the corridor, and banging of trunks, and halting feet on the stairs of them that went down, carrying burdens. As we sat at the hotel door on our car, the object of solicitude somewhat proudly took his place on another such vehicle. An ordinary boy of twelve or so, he swung himself on the rickety car and looked across at us from innocent blue eyes under a thatch of fair hair. Something about him spoke of the mother's boy. His clothes had the look of being made at home by a woman; his scarlet hand-knitted stockings told of maternal care; round his neck, though it was balmy April, a fine muffler was knotted carefully. He swung himself to the well of the car, already laden with luggage and packages, and perched there, with adventurous legs kicking high over the gutters.

"A fine boy, Master Johnny," said our Jehu, half to us, half to himself, with an air of unenvious admiration. "An' the last chick or child herself has by her, barrin' Miss Susy, an' she always that sensible that she's more like the mistress's mother than a slip of a girl. Sure, she's not the same comfort like as Master Johnny." Before we could ask any questions, we heard again the thin sweet voice. It was "Herself," Johnny's mother, standing on the high steps that commanded the street. It was our first introduction to our hostess of last night.

"Did you put in the socks, my sweet-

heart ? " she called to the tow-headed boy.
"And the sandwiches that you'll want in the
railway carriage ?   You haven't forgotten anything, Johnny darling ? "

Johnny grinned somewhat uneasily under
the mother's solicitude.   He was holding his
last audience in the steep street.   Boots, bar-
maid, and chambermaid were gazing at him
from the hall with looks in which sorrow and
admiration were evenly blent.   A crowd of
ragged loafers filled the street, and gathered
about the car.   One could not help thinking
that Johnny might be as well away from
all those zealous understrappers, affectionate
though they seemed.

Johnny's mother presently came out and
climbed the car.   An eager, hectic, handsome
woman, clad all her slender height in decent
black.   She looked like one who had been
long a widow.   Then came a sober-looking
girl with glasses, whom it was easy to recognize
as the jarvey's Miss Susy.   She got up beside
her mother and arranged the parcels in a dull,

K

methodical way. She looked as if she had never been young. I suppose life in a decaying Irish country town is very drab-coloured. Miss Susy's settled dreariness was a strange contrast to her mother's feverishly-eager face.

"He's but a little chap to take the green fields to Amerikay alone. Ay, surely!" said our carman, musingly. By this time we were rattling down the steep street, and over the bridge, from which we could see the silver spray of the falls below, and hear the dull thunder. The other car was close behind, all the ragged retainers trotting cheerfully in its wake. "Is there much emigration from here?" one of us asked. "Ay, surely," said the man; "what else is there for them? Sure there isn't enough to keep the life in the old bodies unless the young goes away to Amerikay, and sends home the money. Och, sure, it's the sorrowful place. If you was here last Wednesday, you'd have seen a trainful starting for Derry. An' the same every Wednesday since March. I don't like

to be about the station myself them times.
It's terrible hard for them to go."

We asked one or two sympathetic questions. He answered us, flicking his whip.
"There's some," he said, "that'll hold up
strong an' silent; an' there's others, again,
keenin' worse than the old women at the
wakes. There's a girl now," he broke off,
pointing at a straight, handsome creature,
who was just stepping across the street:
"There's a girl started for Amerikay, an' kem
home the next day. Ay, faith, it was the
shortest voyage ever known in this town.
She turned back from Derry. Said she
didn't give a *thraneen* for the passage-money.
She'd work her fingers to the bone to earn
enough money to keep the ould woman out of
the workhouse without lavin' her childless."
He said it with a certain admiration, and
added immediately afterwards, "There's not
a handsomer nor cleverer girl than that same
Nancy Goligher in the three baronies."

Then he planted his feet firmly, as if he

K 2

had talked enough, and began to sing in a deep
baritone :

Farewell to Ballyshanny, where I was bred and born,
Go where I may, I'll think of you, as sure as night and
     morn ;
The kindly spot, the friendly town, where every one is
     known,
And not a face in all the place but partly seems my own ;
There's not a house or window, there's not a field or hill,
But east or west, in foreign lands, I'll recollect them still ;
I leave my warm heart with you, though my back I'm
     forced to turn,
So adieu to Ballyshanny and the winding banks of Erne.

It was the song of a townsman, who has won
the delightful immortality of being the ballad-
maker to his birthplace. Under the circum-
stances, the song sounded curiously mournful.

Inside the station, where we all were
presently awaiting the train, a few more
friendly folk came to Johnny's send-off. Miss
Susy stood apart, seemingly indifferent. The
mother talked to a grey old fellow, who
looked like a responsible friend of the family,
of Johnny, and the pity it was the child should
have to take that long, long journey alone.

She was certainly wonderfully handsome. Her skin, for all its fine wrinkles, was delicate as egg-shell china. Her features, of a severe and classical beauty, well matched the transparent colour. Her eyes were large, light blue, and well opened under their large lids. Her eagerness lit up the pale blue orbs, and planted flickering flames of colour in each delicate cheek. Incessantly, as she talked, her eyes went after Johnny. His small luggage was piled about her feet. Now and again a nervous anxiety of some sort would seize her, and she would make a flurried application to her daughter. The quiet girl reassured her monotonously that nothing had been forgotten, that she knew exactly what to do till her mother returned from Derry, and a hundred such things. It was easy to see that the monotony of her daughter's answers fretted the nervous woman.

Johnny meanwhile was holding audience outside the station, being glad to escape, I suppose, from all the talk about him. He swaggered up and down with his hands in his pockets, and we could hear him committing himself to many rash promises of letter-writing. Sometimes he blinked uneasily as if a little salt-water drop troubled his eyesight. After such moments of weakness he swaggered more than before, and shrugged his shoulders with a fine manly impatience as his mother's incessant pity of him fell upon his ear.

The pair got into our railway carriage just before we started. The other occupants were a dried-up American nabob, with a seal-skin coat, and a big brilliant in his scarf-ring, and an acidulated lady of uncertain years, who smiled contemptuously at poor Johnny, and his mother's long-winded solicitude over him. The train went in and out by the banks of an exquisite river; over yonder were the blue lances of the first range of mountains of the glorious hill-country. The American was patronizing over Irish affairs, and very inquisitive. Elucidation was difficult

under the disbelieving smile of the acidulated
damsel.   We could see that Johnny's mother
threw eager glances at the rich American,
and understood that she somehow thought
he might be of use to Johnny.   Her eyes
leaped at him, between spasms of concern
because Johnny would lie half his length
out of the carriage window.   "You see,"
she said to us all, "he's only a very
little boy to be going all the way to
America by himself."   Presently she was
telling it all to us again, going over and over
the phrases I had heard at the railway station.
But what a story of sacrifice and patience!
The woman grew heroic to us, as she sat
there, pouring it out as if it were a common
thing.   Her husband was in Florida eleven
years.   He had gone there alone, when the
needs of a growing family, and the decaying
trade of the town, became serious matters.
Each year one of the children had gone to
him, the mother keeping by her to the last
Susy, the eldest girl, who was wise and

helpful.   Now it had come to the parting with
the very little one, the boy who had been a
child at the breast when his father had last
seen him.   Next year Susy would go ; the
year after, if God spared her, the mother.
We looked at her thin fingers and hectic
cheeks.   " Could you   not go   next year
too ? " some one asked.   She shook her head.
" There would not be the money for two," she
said, " and Johnny's father, though he has toiled
and slaved, is very poor still.   In two years'
time, please God, the hotel will be sold, and
we'll all be under the same roof once more."

She spoke as if two years, to one who had
already ·endured so many, counted little.   It
seemed a sublime patience and hopefulness.
The American looked out at the exquisite
country, and shook his head.   It puzzled
him that there should be such poverty to
override God's precept, that husband and
wife shall not be parted ; and here, in a land
covered with tiny green spears of corn,
dappled with the gold   and white of the

pastures, under such a sky, by such a river, full of the rosy salmon.

Meanwhile Johnny had got used to his mother's complaints. He was sitting with his chin thrust forward, his head somewhat sunk, his unseeing eyes fixed upon the silver river. He was whistling to himself, softly through his half-closed lips. He kept time to his whistling, tapping with his finger on the window pane. It was the song we had heard the carman sing; the song that is in every itinerant street singer's *répertoire* in Bally-shannon :

The thrush will call through Camlin groves the livelong
          summer day ;
The waters run by mossy cliffs and banks with wild
          flowers gay ;
The girls will bring their work and sing beneath a twisted
          thorn,
Or stray with sweethearts down the path among the grow-
          ing corn ;
Along the river side they go, where I have often been—
O never shall I see again the happy days I've seen !
A thousand chances are to one I never may return—
Adieu to Ballyshanny and the winding banks of Erne !

CISSY : AN EXILE.

READING to-day that sketch on which Henry James has spent his exquisite skill, " A Passionate Pilgrim," I was at once reminded of Cissy. Not that she need be out of my mind yet, seeing that it was only on the wet Tuesday of last week they laid her below the tall poplars that are in the boundary hedge of the village graveyard. Brother Dominic, of the Dominicans, who is a Frenchman, had planned her a pretty pageantry. The French convents are the homes of such things —of gauze-winged angels flinging flowers in the path of the priest on Corpus Christi ; of clouds and stars and angels—strange innovations in the usually artless presentation of the Crib ; things that delight much children and innocent persons, such as nuns are, and monks very

often, and peasants nearly always. The children
in white frocks were to carry Cissy from the
bed which had been her patient prison since
she came from India, to that last green bed
which, being Irish earth, must needs have
satisfied her heart-hunger for Ireland. Brother
Dominic is old enough to know better; but he
has not long been over from France, and has
not learned how ill angels in white frocks agree
with an Irish January. Anyhow, the rain came
down in torrents, and the opportunity of
making some of these chubby children into
real angels never came off. I did not see the
poor little funeral, and do not know who were
Cissy's bearers. She was light enough, poor
child—a very featherweight. When I passed
the house later in the evening, a solitary candle
illuminated dully the whitewashed room. There
was no sign of life visible through the uncurtained pane. I imagined the old grandmother
sitting in the corner, her apron over her head,
rocking herself to and fro in the extremity of
her sorrow. The grandfather was outside in

the little garden, his foot on the spade, on the handle of which he leant motionless. In the half-light he looked like an apparition, so still was he. He did not seem to see or hear me going by—I, who was Cissy's friend, and so always welcome to them.

My very first impression of Cissy was from a photograph of her sent home by the proud parents from India. She was then about eight months old. She was a solemn, dark-eyed baby, with a soft down over her head, and extremely well-developed limbs, apparently kicking lustily in front of her, or at least ready to kick. There was not a sign of consumption then. No nursery I know could have furnished forth a more promising baby. The grandfather brought us the picture with pride. It was in a cheap brass frame. I remember that he said, with pretended indignation, " Sorra a thing at all the ould woman will do since it came into the house. She's starin' at it from mornin' till night. I believe she takes it to the bed wid her."

Cissy's mother was their daughter, a wild youngster. I remember her, with brown hair tied with a red ribbon, a wholesome colour, a very wide mouth full of white teeth, innocent dark blue eyes, and a nose so broad and cocked that it sat astride her face. That nose would have been fatal to her good looks in a more advanced state of society. Yet somehow it added to her look of frank good-humour. Then she danced delightfully, as her tall brothers did, and this gave her a certain little position of a belle at the rustic dances. Not only did she move as gracefully as a daffodil on its stalk, but she had by heart the fine science of step-dancing. Seeing Essie in a jig, one forgot her cocked nose, and gave her the generous tribute due to beauty and genius. She danced herself into the heart of a plain-faced, good-natured, young soldier, who had at the time of their marriage earned his corporal's stripes. The more pretentious girls about the place were rather disgusted, especially when a year later Essie came back in a black silk

gown, with a gold watch and chain, as a
sergeant's wife. It was to say good-bye to the
old folk, for Alick had got his orders for India.

I remember what a lady she seemed. She
had acquired a great softness of voice and
manner, and had a certain languor about her
and in her big velvety eyes. She had not
taken kindly to the other women in the
barracks. They were a little too versed in the
shady things of life for this innocent peasant
girl. Their speech and their manners had
only inspired her with a vague horror of them.
Though she had gained that matronly comeli-
ness, her eyes were as innocent as last year,
when she had run wild in the fields, her long
hair streaming. Alick's manner to her pleased
us. I think he was proud of the ladyhood
she had acquired so easily and naturally. She
gave one the impression of a woman who was
cherished.

Cissy was born three months after they
went out. They sent home grand stories of
the climate, and the pay, and of Alick's

promotion, and of the baby's progress. They
were far north in a comparatively cool and
healthful spot of the great Indian Empire.
Years went—well with them, ill enough for
the old people at home. First a son went to
America and was lost sight of. Then the
youngest of the three sons died after a sharp
lung attack caught on a wet winter day. The
eldest son married against the old people's will.
They had something against the girl, though
what I never knew. He died, too, after a
year of married life, and his widow drifted
away to the town. None of Essie's children
lived except Cissy; and the child became as
much the centre of life to the lonely old couple
at home in Ireland as she could be to the
young couple in India. Essie kept them well
informed. The letters, written in her large
straggling hand, were full of things Cissy had
said and done, which the old grand-parents
were never tired of rehearsing. I think they
learnt the letters by heart from hearing them
read, for neither could read. I found the

grandmother one evening sitting crying at the fire, with all the precious letters in her lap. It was a day or two after the old fellow had confided to me that the old woman " was frettin' herself to death for a sight o' the babby." She brightened up when we began to talk; and as she verified this and that anecdote by appeal to the letters, I could see she had every one ranged and sorted and by heart.

So till Cissy was nearly seven years old—a great girl, wrote her mother, and learning sense, and going to be a credit to them all. The Colonel's lady had taken notice of her prettiness, and the regimental schoolmaster prophesied of her cleverness; and so good, said the mother; she knew her prayers by heart, and was taking to the needle, and a good patriot, like Jim, Lord rest him, who was dead and gone. " I do often be wishin'," she wrote, " that she could be playin' in the fields at home. She loves to be hearin' about Ireland. Many a time will she draw her stool beside me an' keep askin' me to tell about

Ireland. Wid the questions she asks I often think she does be thinkin' Ireland's as fine as heaven. An' sure it's heaven it is to them that was born in it, and has to be out of it now."

That was before the regiment moved to the plains. Down there where the barracks stood, amid boundless miles of dust and desert under a pitiless sun, the vision of Ireland so green, and full of waterpools, was like enough to be the heaven of a mirage.

At first Essie wrote bravely enough. Then the heat came, and with it sickness and death. The officers sent their wives and children to the hills. Those who could not do that dreed their lot as best they could. Alick, who was now quartermaster, could have sent Essie and the child to the cooler heights, but Essie would not leave him. Then the child grew puny and fretted. Her cheeks, that had had a soft wholesome paleness, set up two flaming red ensigns. She went about restlessly, with her eyes shining, or else she sat dully, with her

L

chin, that was growing peaked, sunk on her chest. The regimental doctor came and saw her, said she should be sent to the hills or home, and prescribed some simple cooling medicine. Presently she set up a wailing cry. "Mother, let us go home to Ireland! Oh, mother, do let us go to Ireland! I am so hot here; I am so thirsty!" She kept at it with the heart-breaking persistency of a sick child. Then her father and mother saw that if she was to be spared to them she must go home; and Alick got leave to take her up-country to where a regiment was under orders for Ireland, and there to put her in charge of the wife of an old chum.

Essie wrote it all home to the old people with a patient quietness. "I don't know what has come over Cissy," she wrote, "to be so glad to leave us : but she has so moidered us wid questions about when she's goin', and how long it will take to get to Ireland. It vexes her father; but sure she's sick, the creature, and we have filled her head so full of *ramaushes* about Ireland, she thinks she'd never see a sick day if she was once there. She's got Ireland into her head the way other children get heaven or fairyland."

When I read this letter aloud, I looked with a certain apprehension about the little cabin. The walls were blackened with turf-reek then. An uninviting settle-bed was in one corner. There was a pool of mud at the door. The plates on the kitchen-dresser had the smoke of ages on them for the most part. I looked up again at Cissy's last photograph, and read dreams in the big eyes, and noted how above them the forehead was over-big with imagination and ideality. The old woman answered my unspoken thought.

"Sure, Tom's goin' to whitewash for me, plaze God, and fill up that ould hole in the flure. An' Biddy Nugent's comin' in o' Monday to help me wash up and tidy, and have the place elegant for the darlin'."

She did indeed do wonders in her way. The wife of the doctor, who was Tom's employer, helped when she found what was going on. I, too, helped a little. The settle-bed went into "the room," which, being but a little place at the back of the chimney, was warm for the old couple. When the walls were whitewashed and the floor mended, there was not a bad background to work against.. The kitchen-dresser and all its plates shone again. We put lace curtains on the window and a few geraniums in it. An iron bedstead, which the doctor's children had outgrown, was set up in the corner for the sick child. When we were done the place looked clean and comfortable enough.

A little later I was sent for to see Cissy. I expected to find great excitement, but the old grandmother met me at the door with a subdued air. "She's tired after last night, an' lyin' down; but she's awake," she said. The child was lying on the bed when I went in. I was rather shocked. She had the hectic flush of illness, the vivid colour of the consumptive. Her hair was in little red-gold curls, her cheeks vividly red, her eyes intensely blue. She smiled

at me with something of an effort. "She says
she's hot," said the grandmother ; " but awhile
ago I had to be wrappin' her in the blanket,
she was that cold. It's the changes of the
climate do be tryin' her at first." I gathered
that she had been full of excitement and chatter
the night before. Tom had brought her home
in a cab, the night being wet. She had sat in
the grandfather's big arm-chair before a red fire,
and seemed full of happiness. "The longin' is
on her," said the grandmother, "to get out in
the fields. She has seen a little o' them
through the window there, and thinks them
grand." I followed the child's gaze. Outside
a damp autumn mist was curling in the hollows.
The hedges were dark and the fallen leaves
soppy under one's feet. " Cissy must wait," I
said, " for a finer day."

That was my first of many visits. To me it
was evident very soon, even before Dr. Luttrell
had told me, that the child was in a rapid consumption. We got her some things the old
people could not afford. She took nourishment

greedily, as if the weakness were an unbearable
pain. She liked to see me coming with a little
gift. A brown rosary that had travelled to
Jerusalem and touched the Holy Sepulchre
was a precious gift to her. In the latter days
I rarely saw her without it twisted round her
little skinny hand.

The old grandfather and grandmother
thought the spring would make her well. I
never disturbed their delusion. Quiescent
about other things, Cissy had not forgotten
her old dreams of Ireland. She liked to have
me describe things outside for her, as if she
were still in India. I used to come in and tell
her how the mountains looked, and what a sunset there was. "Tell her now, Miss," the old
woman would say, "how the country will look
in May, when the thorn-bushes are out in
flower, and the fields are full of buttercups and
daisies." The child loved these recitals as
children will love a familiar fairy tale, and be
content with no other.

I was away those ten days when she suffered

greatly, and the old people at last gave up hope
that the spring would cure her.   She was dead
when I came back.   I did not see her dead ; I
shrank from the pain of it.   But that evening
of her funeral, when they had laid her in the
grave, was such a sky as in my wildest picture-
painting for her I had not imagined.   The rain
stopped, and the grey sky bloomed into a
splendour of fiery roses—the rose garden of the
sunset, I should have said, only that to east-
ward there were furrows and drifts of the
shining roses : gardens of roses, fields of roses,
a world of roses.   The splendour in the sky
was mirrored in the wet earth.   Every glittering hedgerow blushed rosily.   The west
throbbed like a great mirror reflecting a rosy
fire.   It shone ruddily on the ivy-leaves of the
church tower, where, as I passed, jackdaws
and martins were chattering.   The three
poplar-trees stood up dark and slender against
it.   But Cissy's grave was in shadow when
high in the poplars a blackbird began his full
song of the coming spring.   The ears below

were deaf to his message. Frost and snow, rain and mist, had held the world since the hungry-hearted little exile had come home, but the spring she had not known, though she had desired to see it most of all. She died with her dream of it, and lies at the root of the snowdrops that shall rise to answer its call. Poor little Cissy!

A SPOILT PRIEST.

IN Ireland "a spoilt priest" is a term which carries with it a certain profound contempt. One who has entered at Maynooth for the priesthood, and then relinquished the ecclesiastical for mundane things is popularly supposed to be good for nothing. The same injustice of thought is half-unconsciously dealt out to the woman who has entered a convent, and left it finding she has mistaken her vocation. Mrs. McNelis had these feelings to an exaggerated extent, so, to her, it was a bitter pill indeed when her son, Hugh, with the courage of despair, announced his unalterable resolve never to become a priest. Yet in the first bitterness I doubt that she quite gave up her cherished hope for lost, or really believed that Hugh, whom she had moulded like wax between her fingers through his length of days, would continue to uphold his will against hers.

No doubt she loved the boy after her fashion. She was a terrible old woman, straight-backed, stern-featured, with eyes of cold blue set in her colourless face—a woman who had not known ache, pain, or moral backsliding, as she understood it, and was as pitiless to the helpless or sinning of this world, as she would be to a lame chicken or a recalcitrant puppy. "Away with it!" she would say. Hugh all his life had been trained under sternest rule and discipline. Whatever his character might have been if it had been allowed to follow its natural bent, there was no doubt that now it had some defect of weakness. He was a brown-eyed, pleasant-faced boy, with a sweet mouth, his father's son every inch of him. The marriage of his parents had not been a happy one. His father too, I suppose, had Hugh's pliancy. Anyhow, he was quite young when the marriage was made for him, and it was usual enough among his people to let the old folk settle matters, while the intending bride and groom were but more or less interested spectators. The result in this union was that the elder Hugh McNelis equally feared and hated his dark-browed, handsome wife, while she elbowed him aside to take the lead in all things, and regarded him with a mingled tolerance and contempt.

Mrs. McNelis was a very devout woman, though she missed out all the love that is the heart of religion. She should have been a Jew of old, or a worshipper at some very fierce and narrow Little Bethel. She liked sermons on Judgment and Hell, and only tolerated the gentler pronouncements of the priests because they happened to proceed from priests. As a Catholic she was out of place, for the Catholic religion is one that insists more than any other on the Love of God. Holding the priesthood in enormous veneration, she had destined Hugh from the hour he was born to be a priest. She was a prosperous hotel-keeper in a country town, and therefore the giving of her one child

to the Church would be by many esteemed a
sacrifice. But this old woman would have been
amazed at the idea of sacrifice. There was
something heroic, though hopelessly wrong, in
her passionate purpose to make a priest of
Hugh. Just as readily would she stand by
glorying to see him burnt at the stake for his
faith's sake. Just as readily would she herself
walk upon burning ploughshares, or endure the
rack, the pincers, or the thumbscrew. She
would have suffered for her faith quite as
readily as she would have persecuted for it.

She would probably have had her will with
Hugh but for an unforeseen happening. Many
most admirable priests must have acquired
their vocation rather than received it. His
mother kept the idea before him through all
his childhood, so that he never thought of
disputing it. The little town is among heroic
scenery, holy with heroic memories. North-
ward the saw teeth of a great range of mountains divide lowland and highland. To stand
in the town street and look at them in the dis-

tance makes one's heart beat; they suggest such a glorious country beyond. It is glorious indeed. One enters it by a long pass heaped high with stones a race of giants might have used in their games; they are set with great symmetry, one upon the other, as though the giants had had a play of housebuilding as a child builds a card castle, being tired of hurley, putting the stone, and the other old strong games. In the highland country it is miles and miles of desolate glens or mountain ranges, or great bleak hills dreaming in solitary grandeur. There is Muckish with slanting sides like a house roof, and Slieve League with a giant face in stone gazing sternly from its summit into the quiet heaven, and Errigal, and many others nearly as great, but with no names to call them by. It was a great fighting country long ago. Elizabeth's men might ravage Munster, and leave famine, like the locusts, where they had found green pastures, but before this wall of the North they sat helpless and afraid.

The place and its memories are full of inspiration for the generous time of youth. Even such thoughts in her son Mrs. McNelis discouraged harshly. The heroism of martyrs and missionary priests was the one heroism for her. Hugh was trained, slightly against the grain, to be quiet and prayerful. In due time he went to Maynooth, and gave none of his professors any uneasiness about him in the first year of his course.

He said afterwards, that as his mind opened to all the priesthood involved, he became dissatisfied ; but that was a mood which, passing, might have left him all the more ready to receive the true vocation. However, the summer vacation of that year settled the question for ever. He was looking a little pale when he came home, and his mother, more tender to him than she had ever shown herself before, suggested after a while that he should make an expedition into the mountains and settle for a week or two at a little town on the wild North coast, where the

Atlantic comes in under a frowning great Head, and the people are all fisher folk or sailors. In this town lived a cousin of his father's, of whom the old woman entertained a poor opinion. Yet she thought as a matter of duty that Hugh should see him when in the town. Mrs. McNelis had certainly placed her husband's business and position far beyond what he could ever have done for himself, good easy man. But while Hugh McNelis had prospered Jerry McDonnell had stood still, or perhaps had been a little retrograde. His wife, Sabina, a soft creature, as Mrs. McNelis called her contemptuously, was dead. There was a household of daughters, she had heard somehow or other, but it was an acquaintance she had not cared to follow up; and indeed neither Jerry McDonnell nor Sabina were ever tempted to intrude on their repellant cousin-in-law.

Hugh settled down among his new-found relatives with an ease that would have disgusted his mother. The warmth and love that was between father and daughters warmed poor Hugh like a fire when one comes in out of cold rain. Alice, the eldest girl, was my friend whom I knew in Dublin. Long after, in their own country, I asked two or three people whether the other girls were like Alice. " Just as good, as gentle, as charming," said one melancholy old lady; a remark corroborated by carmen and others to whom I spoke, in rather different language. It was hard to believe there could be more than one such girl in an Irish village. Alice was an exquisite motherly creature, and had mothered both her father and her sisters after her own mother died. I have seen her setting her father's blue tie straight or brushing away the dust from his coat sleeves as, stick in hand, he set out on some expedition, doing the little common offices with a grave tenderness that suggested pity and love and watchfulness, all combined. The maternal in a motherly woman is not kept for one love only. It embraces all things, and perhaps male creatures especially, in its great pity. Alice used to treat the little girls as if they were her own children. What work there was with them at the common going-forth to school; and more than that at the great function of Sunday morning before she brought her demure little flock to mass, with their Leghorn hats and grey frocks, sailing down the windy street like pretty little craft at sea. She loved those children so much that before Hugh McNelis came to Ardmore they filled her peaceful heart. It was a heart that loved duty, and when afterwards, on a somewhat flimsy pretence, she ran away to Dublin and settled there all one winter, it but proved to me how absorbing was the new love that for the time pushed all those gentle ones out of the first place in her heart.

How the love began who can say? It was Alice's way to be very kind, and the boy, so simple and gentle, who seemed years younger than herself, and who turned to the kindness that was the law of the

M

house as eagerly as a long-darkened flower
turns to the sun, appealed to her strongly.
The fact that he was destined for the priesthood set her on easier terms with him.   There
was no reason why she should not sit for
hours with her pile of household sewing,
listening to the thoughts so long pent up
that flowed eagerly to this interested listener.
Sometimes it was beside the window filled
with flower-pots that they sat, Alice with
her basket of stockings or linen to be
mended beside her ; the young fellow, lounging
all his length in an easy chair, watching her
bent head and her fingers moving swiftly.
Or, if the weather was unusually propitious
and the Atlantic breakers basking all their
length like sleeping lions, Hugh would carry
his cousin's basket up to the cliffs over the
sea, . where the rocks made many sheltered
places, and the lichened boulders provided
seats for all comers.   I saw one of their
haunts in April : it was an enchanted glade
of tall ferns and nodding blue-bells, a place

where the fairies dance in moon-white nights.
Knowing Alice and her charming face, I
could picture her so well, with the red-gold
hair lifted back from her little ears, her soft
and changing colour and her velvety blue eyes,
full of a light of kindness. No wonder the
young fellow fell in love with her.

Whether she loved him then I do not
know. The very idea of the priesthood as
associated with the boy was pretty sure to
keep her conscious thoughts a thousand miles
away from love. He himself knew his own
case well, and guessed, perhaps, that it would
be easy to turn the girl's exquisite kindness to
love, if once the bar between them were
removed. He said nothing to her, however,
while he wore the garb of a divinity student.
He went home fully wound up to confront
his mother.

The storm swept him off his feet. His
mother was far more terribly wrathful than
even he had feared. He had not meant
to tell her about Alice ; but she divined

M 2

something of the truth, and, once brought to bay, he brazened it out piteously. To her the whole thing was as if one had rejected the service of God for the service of sin. The girl who innocently had defeated her purpose seemed in her eyes worse than a Jezebel. Her grey fury fairly frightened the boy out of his wits. Standing, confronting him, with one lean finger pointing, her words hissed at him like curses. For two or three days their wills wrestled, but it was a foregone conclusion that the fight should fall to the strongest. By the end of the week Hugh McNelis had given in, temporizing with the fatal weakness that had grown up in him, and had consented to sail to Spain, there to continue his ecclesiastical studies at the college of Salamanca.

Once he was gone Mrs. McNelis forgave him; but such a hatred grew up in her for the girl who had decoyed her son away from his vocation, that all that autumn she grew yellower, bitterer, more uncompromising. She nursed her wrongs in her own bosom, and I doubt that even the confessor to whom she told her lapses from the path of her terrible rectitude, knew anything of the resentment that was corroding her iron heart. But there was a worse blow in store for her. One fine day before Christmas Hugh returned to her, walking into her private room, where she sat casting up her accounts, in an ordinary secular garb, which horrified her eyes as much as if it had been a convict's black and yellow. He looked ill and weary, and little fitted for a new tussle with her. He handed her silently a letter, which she read in a silence as grim as death. It was from the President of the College, telling her in polite Spanish terms that the young gentleman had mistaken his vocation, and how much they regretted that they could not have the further direction of his studies. She looked at him in a stony silence. " Do you mean to marry that girl ? " she said at last. Hugh answered her wearily. " If she will have me and wait for me ; she knows nothing of all this." His mother pointed to the door:

"Carry your disgrace to her, then," she said, "for you are no son of mine." The lad looked at her in wonder; he was fagged after a long journey, and had neither eaten nor drunk; his head reeled with fatigue and want of food. The colourless face told him that she meant what she said. He stood up and took his hat, and with a depressed droop of the head and shoulders, left his mother's presence.

He was not to go quite hopeless and un-comforted. As he went down the stairs a friendly hand was laid on his. "Glory be to God, Master Hugh," said Barney, the boots and general factotum of the hotel; "sure it's not lavin' your mother's house you are, widout bit or sup." "She has turned me out, Barney," said the boy bitterly. "God forgive her, the ould naygur," said Barney, under his breath; and then, in a coaxing voice, as if Hugh were a very small child, "sure it's only her tantrums, Master Hugh, an' it's sorry she'll be for it. But you won't go hungry, anyhow."

So in Barney's little room beside the stables Hugh was fed and refreshed.

It was a long drive on the mail car to Ardmore, and when Hugh walked into Jerry McDonnell's fire-lit parlour he looked cold and ill. Alice was alone, for the little girls were all up at the Convent helping to dress the Christmas tree. She was sitting in the half-light knitting rapidly, with her eyes far away, and the firelight on her bent head and black gown. Before she could ask any question he answered the surprise in her eyes. He knelt on the hearthrug beside her, and put his aching forehead on her lap, "I've put off the priest's coat for ever, Alice," he said, "and my mother has turned me out." I do not pretend to know all that happened, but I can imagine that, seeing her boy in great need, Alice would lean over him and stroke his hair, and caress his tired forehead with her cool fingers till the ache had passed away. I think he made no more declaration of his love than that helpless putting his head upon her knees.

He was ill for several days after that, but be sure Alice coaxed him back to health. I wish the story were different for the poor young things. If it were only a story and not a transcript from life I would make it begin to end happily now. When Hugh was well again he went off to Dublin to study medicine. There was no chance for him but to work by day for his bread, and at night to attend the night schools, which at that time were thronged by eager students. After a little he got a place in a chemist's shop, and then began the rather melancholy performance of burning the candle at both ends.

It went on for a year and a half. In the beginning of the next winter Alice came to Dublin, having got employment at the teaching of lace-making to a class of girls under some industrial scheme. It was then I came to know her, and after a time, having grown to love her, I heard of her poor little love-affair. Her clients at the lace-making rapidly increased; she was really the most charming creature, and seemed to touch irresistibly all manner of people. She got work in some Convent schools and was in a way of being fairly prosperous. She was happy too, being absorbed in her lover and the care of him. His pittance at the chemist's scarcely did more than pay his fees and for his books. He might have starved to death in a Dublin garret that winter if it were not for Alice. I used to think them a pathetic couple. Every evening they were together for an hour, between the closing of the chemist's shop and the opening of the Medical School. Be sure I never intruded on them willingly; but I remember one evening coming in by accident. The tea-table was laid cosily for two, with the addition of a fowl and fresh eggs to the *menu*. Alice was sitting on the floor toasting bread. McNelis was lying in the arm-chair with an air of extreme content; though even then he was thinner than one liked to see him.

They were near each other all that winter. Alice was living with kind people who knew about the love-affair and were sincerely interested in the poor lovers. Mrs. McNelis made no sign—not even when Hugh wrote a letter to her at Christmas.

It was in spring, Alice first told me she was anxious about Hugh. He had contracted a cough in the winter which he found it hard to shake off. Working by day and reading by night were telling on his constitution. As the summer went on I grew anxious about Alice herself. The hot city summer was cruel on the mountain-and-sea-bred girl. The two of them looked rather parched when they used to come to me sometimes for a Sunday in the country, but they were still pathetically happy in being together. In the autumn, Alice told me that Hugh had been asked to take some one's place temporarily as doctor's assistant and compounder on an Atlantic steamer. She was eager that he should accept it, for the sea-trips, she thought, were the very thing he needed to set him up. He was not anxious himself to go. He was so fond of her that he would never have left her side if she had not pushed him out into the world. He sailed with the steamer, and for a time I heard good reports of him. Then Alice came and told me one day that he had been offered something advantageous in New York, and that he had decided to take it, at least temporarily. She was somewhat fearful about him by this time, as women will be when the men they love are not under their own eyes; and I had to laugh her out of her fears, though, Heaven knows, she had all my sympathy.

I don't like lingering over this sad time. In October news came from Hugh that he was ill. Alice gave me the letter without a word when I went to see her after a few weeks' of absence. She looked at me with heavy mournful eyes. The letter was most pathetic. The boy had evidently tried to write bravely, but in every word was a longing for her presence and help far more touching than if he had spoken fully. I asked her if she had done anything. "Yes," she replied, in a dull way; "I did what I never thought to do: I wrote to his mother and implored her to give me money to go to him; she has never answered me." I thought of a dozen schemes for raising the money while I sat there holding her poor hand. It could have been done, no doubt, but before we could do more than move in the matter we heard, indirectly, that Mrs. McNelis herself had gone out to Hugh.

It was curious how Alice took this bit of news. She raged like a young tigress when first it was told to her. Her jealous love was up in arms against the cruel mother, who having reduced him to this, had now once again come between them. But after a time she said she was glad that he would not be alone, nor without care. I was glad when she made up her mind to go home. It was miserable for her in Dublin now the short winter days were closing in, and the streets were murky with fog and rain. She had suffered enough, my poor Alice. Mrs. Barry, the kind woman in whose house she lived, did her best to take care of her. When she came in from her lacemaking—for still she went mechanically to her work—her dinner was given to her in her own little room, beside a cheerful fire. Mrs. Barry explained to me that she was sure the greatest kindness was to leave Alice alone as much as possible. The good woman had tears in her eyes as she told me how sorrowful it was to see the girl in those days when first she heard Hugh was ill. " To see her crumbling the bread and trying to swallow it, and all the time feeling as if every bit would choke her, the creature, would break your heart. And then the watching for the post. I declare I couldn't look at her when we heard the postman's knock coming down the street, for I knew how every drop of blood in her body was listening. And the dead sick look of disappointment when he passed by or brought her nothing. God keep my little girls from the like." And then Mrs. Barry furtively

wiped away her honest tears with the corner
of her apron.

Of the rest of the sad little story I have no
personal cognizance. Alice was quite silent
after her return to the North, and feeling
that she was in such bitter trouble I did
not keep writing letters to her. For many
years now I have heard nothing directly from
her, and it was only last April I was told how
her love-story ran through that mournful winter
and spring.

She went home at least to great love, and to
that tender silence which is the most comprehensive sympathy. Jerry McDonnell might
be a poor creature from a worldly point of view,
but the finest gentleman that ever lived could
not have bettered him in the delicate kindness
he showed his unhappy daughter. When that
mournful pilgrimage of hers, which took place
daily for many months, was going on, he never
asked a question. He saw Alice go away on
the mail-car every evening and return every
morning, dull and fagged, and except for an

added tenderness, there was no sign that this was out of the way. Delia, the second girl, who blooms more rosy than Alice ever was, took the reins of housekeeping while Alice slept or rested in her bedroom up in a gray wind-swept gable. Her father knew that she went every night over sixteen long miles of country to nurse the dying lover, and made no protest. Not even when the weather grew fierce, and she became the only passenger by the mail-car. He bought her a fine fleecy shawl, and used to wrap her in it every evening on the car with a kindness that brought tears to her hot eyes. But he said nothing ; and indeed many hearts as well as his ached with sympathy for the forlorn girl. It was significant of the esteem she was held in that no one seemed to think the proceeding unseemly, though the Irish are so conventional a people. There was nothing but a profound pity and sympathy for her, that survives even to this day, when the story of her past wraps her about like a widow's veil.

Mrs. McNelis had brought her son home to his father's house. There was no doubt of her love for him, for when she came back from America with her dying boy, people said she was scarcely recognizable, she had grown so old, so haggard and weak. Her unbending stature had sunk by a couple of inches. Her fierce old eyes had taken a look of misery. She procured for Hugh the best doctors, and every thing else money could buy. The doctors confirmed the verdict of the local man, that Hugh's illness was consumption, rapid and hopeless. She would give him all things but one, and that was the society of the girl he loved. Against Alice her old implacable hatred had increased a thousand-fold. She looked on her as the cause of all her troubles, of her alienation from her son, his illness, his death that was coming swiftly.

Fortunately for the two whose last solace was to be together, the trouble had broken the old woman's strength. All day she might be about the sick room, but at night she was fain

to leave Hugh to other hands. The hotel servants, who were devoted to him from boyhood,
were supposed to sit up with him. But every
night, as soon as his mother was safely in bed,
the slender black-robed figure of his sweetheart
stole in, and all the night she was near him,
praying, smoothing his pillows, surrounding
him with every tender care, and making his
path to the grave, as far as might be, a happy
one. She came in the dusk of the evening;
she stole out in the grey dawn of the morning.
The hotel servants were banded together to
keep the lovers' secret from the implacable
old mother. All the town knew the story, but
the sympathy being universally with the lovers,
no eavesdropper or spy carried stories. I doubt
that the old woman ever knew to her dying
day how her son's death-bed had been comforted. In the end he died in Alice's arms,
one chilly dawn when the first spring birds
were trilling their unaccustomed notes.

I passed through the little town where she
lives in April. The driver of the mail-car

magnanimously offered me seven minutes in
which to see her, but I could not spring upon
her so suddenly, a ghost out of her dead past.
As I sat while he changed the horses I saw,
in the grey gabled house at the corner, a
figure by the window with a graceful bent
head.   Perhaps it was Alice still mending the
house-linen as in the old days when Hugh
McNelis fell in love with her.   She has a
beautiful reputation in her own country-side,
a reputation of a dutiful daughter, a most
loving and maternal sister, a tender friend and
helper, and outside it all the consecration of her
sad story.   While I sat, the figure at the window
never raised its head.   If it had I am sure
I should have seen Alice's face, less like a
wild rose than of old, but with an exceeding
tender beauty on it of faith, and hope, and love.

WAIFS.

THE Irish country lay sleeping in Sabbath stillness. The hills had retired behind warm mists, out of which flashed here and there a fire like a beacon; weeds or furze burning that transfused the veils of the mist to golden, and made a new beauty in the placid evening. There was a rich sunset. The dews hung in fiery drops on every grass blade; Stellaria and speedwell made drifts of blue and white in the ditches; and the first pearly buds of the hawthorn were bursting their little green shells. Exquisite weather, with a golden tranquillity that seemed to quiet even the cattle. They browsed in the yellow and white pastures with a low sound of feeding that but made silence audible. Very lovely is that Irish country; and the bark of a distant dog, the subdued hum of the city by the far sea-shore, and the bell floating its thought of prayer over the browning meadows, were but sounds that made harmony in the music of its quietness.

We came along a road where the catkins were withering off the willows, and all the marsh marigolds were out in the trenches. For a good Irish mile around there was only a lodge we vaguely guessed to be inhabited, to bring us in touch with the human world. The lodge belonged to an empty house. There are scores such round Dublin going to rack and ruin, the sweetbriar hedges of their gardens trampled through by cattle; the roses returning to a wild state; the fruit a prey to any venturesome urchin who will brave the awe that hangs about a desolated house, to gather it. The land, which so near the city has an artifical value, is in the hands of a farmer, who would if he could, raze the old house to the earth, and bid grass to grow on the hearthstone around which a family had gathered.

We were coming close to the lodge of the

empty house. Just there the road sinks between high thorn hedges, after passing which one climbs the hill again into the world. There is an avenue of beech and elm to the old house. Behind it the sunset shows gorgeously through the arches and pillars, and beyond the bold, springing branches of the trees. As we came along, the frogs were croaking in the ditches, and all the dewy banks were covered with snails out for exercise. As we came near the sinking in the road we saw sitting by the roadside the quaintest, strangest wee figure. If I had been alone, the creature at such an hour and place would have startled me. It sat by the roadside buried in the grass and wearing to all appearance the conical cap of the fairies. My companion laughed, half-scaredly. "What is it?" she said, creeping closer to me. "Is it a leprechaun?"

Our dog shared our distrust. As he noticed the thing he erected his ears and growled suspiciously. Then he crept cautiously before us in a way he has when he suspects anything to be uncanny. Presently taking his courage in both paws, so to speak, he galloped straight up to the little fairy and inspected it. A child's cry of terror reassured him and us. It was indeed a preternaturally small child, who, after that cry of distress, sat with grimy fingers thrust in each eye, and resolutely refused to look at us or answer our questions. He was so unlike a child of the country people that we never associated him with the lodge, which was close at hand. We thought he must have strayed somehow. There had been a gipsy caravan in the neighbourhood, and he looked, with his queer shrivelled appearance, as if he might be some little acrobat, whose tiny limbs were withered by many contortions. We looked towards the lodge in vague distress. There was no firelight in the uncurtained windows; the chimneys were black and smokeless; the place looked quite forlorn, though I had heard there were people living there.

However, our doubts were solved. From the fields where the mists were blotting out the sunlight came an eerie and mournful sound of crying. We looked at each other; it was as if we had suddenly stepped from our safe, pleasant country, every inch of which we knew, into mysteries. Such things had happened to people who stray at eve into fairy raths, but we were not yet quite prepared to accept our leprechaun and the ghostly crying as unreal. While we waited developments the little boy took his yellow fists out of his eyes. " It's Alice," he said, with an unmistakable sigh of relief ; "she went away from me an' Biddy, but she's coming back."

The sound came nearer, drearily along the winding "passway," as they call it, which was once a right of way, but is now choked in parts with briars and thorns. It leads one a very lonely way through the fields, wide fields eerily lonely when the evening comes down. Presently the owner of the wailing voice issued in the roadway, and came nearer, scarcely hushing her monotonous wail even for the surprise of seeing us engaged with the

little brother. Her crying had a strange
meaning for a wee dot like her. It was a
wail of utter despair and weariness, as of
one worn out with trouble, to whom monotonous crying brought relief. The child
could scarcely be more than six, yet her
face was old and tired and lined with
responsibility. Her crying was unaccompanied
by tears, and the dry-eyed grief added
to the intensity of that unchildlike trouble.
She only stopped crying when one of us put a
hand on her head. "What is the matter, little
one?" we said. She looked at first as if she
would not answer. Then she said with hesita-
tion, "Mother went away a long time ago, and
I was frightened, and Jimmy and Biddy were
hungry." "Where is she gone?" we asked.
"She went away over the fields," she answered,
"and father went first, and they never came
back." We asked where they lived. She
pointed her finger to the lodge in the distance.
"Is there no one in the house?" we said.
"Biddy is," she replied; "I was going home

to her. She'll be lonely without Jimmy or me. Come along, Jimmy," she said to the little lad.

We went along the road, a party of four. Jimmy, now he was no longer friendless, trotted along with the happy confidence that belongs by right to his three years of age. Alice had his hand in hers, but there was no corresponding dance in her footstep. She walked heavily, as if already accustomed to carrying burdens. By this time we were tolerably well able to identify the missing father and mother. We had been out through the long hours of the April afternoon, and had met, three or four hours earlier, a man on the road to the village. We noticed that he was slightly drunk from his flushed face. By the hand he held a little chap, who was no doubt the brother of Alice and Jimmy, and who stepped out bravely in the effort to keep up with the man's pace, not at all slackened for his little feet. Half an hour later, as we sat on a bank of violets, two women came by. One was a tall, handsome, sullen-looking girl.

Beside her walked an old crone, with a suspiciously red face and a pair of bleared eyes. She was listening to some story the girl poured out in a shrill vehement voice, with acute sympathy. The girl herself, whom we took to be the mother of these poor babies, was flushed and excited. She looked as if she had been quarrelling with some one, and as the two went by us a reek of whisky floated on the sweet air. Evidently the husband and wife had quarrelled over their drinking, and each had then set out to stupefy themselves anew. We thought the pair of women might have appeared in a picture to be called "Evil Counsel." The passionate, handsome young woman, and the old crone listening, sympathizing, leading the way to the village tavern, where she herself had so often drowned her sorrows and disgrace, were very suggestive.

We comforted Alice as well as we could. In the lodge all was cold and dark. We were very uncertain as to whether Biddy was an old woman, a child, a cat, a hen, or what not ;

so we entered the low door with some curiosity. There was nothing visible that could be Biddy. There was no fire on the black hearth. An empty kettle lay on its side on the floor. Under the window a miserable bed was un-made, and heaped with nondescript garments. There was some broken crockery on the dresser. Sign of food there was none, not even a can of well-water in the wretched hovel.

Alice was evidently concerned at Biddy's non-appearance. She had expected to find her in the bed. She gazed at it with a blank incredulous look. Then she lifted the clothes, and looked under them ; she peered beneath the bed ; she looked into the little empty room that was off the first room. Then she blinked at us with a gaze of helpless bewilderment. Before we could answer her look I chanced to turn round. There was a great stone behind the gate, evidently intended for a rough seat. On this stone was squatted a naked year-old baby as yellow and wrinkled as a little heathen idol. The creature stared at us with round bright eyes, but made absolutely no sound or motion. I laughed out : the little thing was so odd. But Alice, when she saw it, ran at it, with an inarticulate maternal cry, and hugged it up in her arms. She sat down on the stone seat and held the baby against her narrow little chest, folding round it the tiny rag of shawl she was wearing. While we watched, Jimmy too crept up on the stone seat. He had evidently forgotten his hunger, for he sidled around his sister and began to coo to Biddy. Biddy was not the smiling sort ; but a pleasurable excitement came into her little yellow visage, and she caught at the fingers extended to her. Then the pair began a game of hide-and-seek, and we were forgotten. But Alice sat in the midst of it with the mournful responsibility in her big eyes, and the strange gravity on her little dark face. She never joined in the play, but now and again she looked down at the younger children with a brooding maternal sweetness in her grave gaze. I thought how if the group had been seen by a great painter, he would have made of it an immortal picture.

We asked Alice some questions about the cruel father and mother. She answered us with the most guarded air of reservation. It was as if on this strange little one had fallen not only the burden of maternal care for the younger children, but also the maternal need of sheltering from scandal or reproach her unhappy parents. The loyal little soul would say nothing against them. I fear she even perjured herself to shelter their reputations, unwitting all the time that she herself and the forlorn little group of which she was the centre, made the strongest indictment against them.

We went up the hill when the evening star was in the sky, and from a motherly woman begged bread and milk for the poor babes. Her one little son, his father's idol, was learning unsteadily to travel from the settle to his father's knee. They gave their food gladly, and were full of eager sympathy, but were fearful to meddle or to see us meddling. "O Miss, dear," said the gentle little mother, "don't let Bryan an' the wife find you there when they come home, for when the drink is on them, there's no knowing what they'd say or do. God help the poor childher! Sure my heart bleeds for them, an' it's glad I'd be to cuddle them up at the fire with my own Neddy; but it's frightened I'd be of the father an' mother."

I had forgotten the people, but remembered then that Bryan had been in my father's employment at the time he was married. His wife was a handsome, undisciplined creature, almost a child, and came from some unknown source. Some people said her father and mother were gipsies; and anyhow she had the swarthy beauty of the gipsies. Mrs. Keogh, hugging her own little son, had no very stern condemnation of her. "God help her, the crature!" she said; "she was right good till Jim began to beat her. Och, he's the brute when he has the drink taken. An' Molly was

always that proud, that it nearly drove her mad
for him to lift his hand to her. An' so she
took to drownin' her sorrows herself, the
crature. An' they do say, Miss, that that ould·
Mrs. Lloyd that rared her, is to blame for
leadin' her into evil ways. Och, God forbid
I'd blame the poor thing! an' they say she's
kind to the childher, even when she has drink .
taken, an' would kill Bryan if he lifted his hand
to them."

When we went back with Mrs. Keogh's
bread and milk, Jimmy and Biddy were asleep,
curled up about the elder child, who sat grave
and unwinking, gazing at the procession of the
stars that was filing down the sky. She roused
up the sleepy-heads and fed them, not taking
bit or sup herself till they were satisfied. We
left them so in the warm spring night; April
this year was warm as June; and for long I·
heard no more of them. Next day I left home
for a tour through a wild Northern country,
and only returned to pack up my things for a
flitting, "for good," as they say.

Poor little waifs! I have often thought of
them. I heard the other day the mother was dead.
The father drinks worse than ever.   Perhaps
now the mother is better to them.   I knew in
that wild Northern country a family of mother-
less bairns, just such helpless weans as Alice,
Jimmy and Biddy. The father was a drunkard.
The children, left alone three nights out of
four, were for some time a scandal to the
parish, so great was their dirt and misery.   All
of a sudden they appeared one fine morning
washed and bright, with their little yellow curls
smoothed like silk. The neighbours marvelled.
Some curious person interrogated the children.
"Mother came," they said, "dressed in white,
and kissed us and cried.   And then she fed us
and washed us and went away."   And no one
could shake them in their story, even though
they were confronted with that high tribunal,
the parish priest.   But their father was so sure
of the truth of the story that it changed him
entirely, and he became a sober, God-fearing
man and a most tender father.   Perhaps it is

not a solitary case. It might well be that the barriers of another world, of death and the grave, would not be strong enough to keep away from her desolate babies a dead mother who knew them neglected and ill-treated.

A DESCENDANT OF IRISH EARLS.

HE sat in my little room on a brilliant day of May, despite that he wore a working-man's respectable cheap suit of tweeds, in face and gaze a reverend signior. The light blue eyes, that had just a film of dreams upon them, regarded me with grave dignity. The long slender olive face, with its finely-pointed beard, was the ideal one for doublet and ruff. Clap the head in an ancient picture frame, and place it alongside a gallery's length of Desmond's Earls, and you would at once recognize the relationship. Certainly not a pretender, and still less, one thought, marking his air of quiet belief in his assertions, a man who pretended to himself, or inwardly fell short of his pretensions. I suppose *noblesse oblige* will bind, or may bind, as surely the inheritor

of proud blood and traditions fallen to a trade
of glass-making, as one yet in possession of his
inheritance.   I do not know if my poor friend
was a glass-blower *manqué* because of his
Desmond blood ; but sure am I that his
dreams wove in the crystals such magic lines of
rose and opal that if such things were tangible
he were a finer craftsman than the finest of
Salviatis. Sitting at his work I make no doubt
he blew glass—and other things.   Fairy
iridescent things that floated between earth and
sky, and had in them the glory of a prism.
But presently he must needs go home to the
tall tenement house in a grimy Dublin street,
where wife and weans were depending on his
mere prosaic glass-making; and there, no doubt,
the poverty, the crying children, the poor room,
would prick that rosy bubble that had floated
home with him along the dark streets.

In Dublin one is not often out of sight of
the mountains, nor out of smell of the sea. At
least these things are nearly always easy to
regain. From upper .windows one can get a

glimpse of the blue hills, these spring days glorified with the rose and purple of the East wind. These same East-windy mornings the salt breath of the sea comes up through the streets, reminding one delightfully that Dublin is a seaboard city. G—— Street, however, though the tenements be leaning over from height and ricketiness, affords one no glimpse of the mountains ; and though a five minutes' walk will bring you in sight of Howth, like a sapphire in the bay, the sea-strand you will come upon is little more than mud-banks and sewage deposit, and from that blows no sea-salt, bright and sweet.

On the street itself is writ large, as with many of its neighbours, *Ichabod.* These were the dwellings of the peers and gentlemen-commoners of Ireland in the palmy days before the Union, the days that no legislation will restore, any more than it will " The glory that was Greece, and the grandeur that was Rome." The houses have forlorn remnants of bygone splendour. Doors and window-shutters are of

wine-red mahogany, rich and ancient.   Ornate
decorations in Italian stucco-work are on walls
and ceiling.   Why, here Angelica Kauffmann
may have worked herself, for she came over
in that reign of splendour, the Rutland Vice-
royalty, to decorate some of these houses, the
Irish nobility having singularly munificent
ideas about decoration, and the best artists
to perform it.

It was of a Bank-holiday my Desmond
visited me.   Any other day he had been at his
glass-blowing.   I suppose it was delightful to
him to get out of the dark street, and come by
lanes of bloomy hawthorn, and fields of white
and gold, with scarce a grass-blade between,
and to find at the end of that delightful journey
—sympathy.   I suppose the wife was a little
intolerant of her earl-presumptive.   I am sure
the children were, especially the two elder
ones, a boy and a girl grown enough to be
employed respectably as a post-office sorter
and an apprentice to the dressmaking, respec-
tively.   After all, when one is earning one's

money, and well-content with the state of life
in which God has placed one, it is somewhat
irritating to have a father who is a pseudo-
earl, and with very serious ideas of the ways
and manners incumbent on one because
there is in one's veins the blood of nobles,
saints and warriors, who are come to be less
than dust, and of no possible use to their
descendants.

He came to me for sympathy because he
had seen an article of mine about Youghal,
once the seat of the Desmond power, in which
I had been enthusiastic over that great line—a
line rather of Irish princes than of Anglo-Irish
earls.   Between them and their cousins, the
Kildare Fitzgeralds, they pretty well halved
Ireland.   Indeed all the great Southern and
Eastern expanse of Ireland would have been
theirs, except for a race sprung from a plaguy
fellow who was Henry the Second's butler, and
had founded a race of Butlers, great in brain-
power as well as in thew and sinew.   These
and the Fitzgeralds hated each other with a

bitter rivalry. However, my Fitzgerald of
Desmond thought upon me as one likely to
understand what he had inherited.   And,
poor soul, he had grown tired of trying to air
in the columns of newspapers—mostly closed
to him as a poor bore—the fact that he was
the lineal descendant of the great Earls of
Desmond, and that he would like to know on
what basis certain ladies of wealth and position
rested their claims to dispossess him of his
honours.

He had come to prove his claims to one
interested listener.   Therefore he waved away
all offer of refreshment; and producing from
an old portfolio, which he carried as if it con-
tained the Crown jewels, various documents,
he demanded my attention for them.   Each
was tied and folded with scrupulous care; each
wrapped in layers of tissue-paper.   They were
worn so thin that they needed such protection.
" I am in the habit of perusing them frequently,
madam," he said in his formal manner, and
gazing at me over his great spectacles.   It was

easy to see that by the way he followed from a distance my reading of the MSS.

There was an elaborate and careful account of his derivation from Garrett Fitzgerald, nineteenth Earl of Desmond, and his wife Helen, daughter of Lord Richard Condon.   His grandmother, Elizabeth Fitzgerald, was the grand-daughter of this last Fitzgerald to bear the title of Earl Desmond.   They were three forlorn damsels, Elizabeth, Elleanora, and Helen, tricked of their inheritance as effectually as was their ancestor in 1589, by Sir Walter Raleigh, who was himself stript bare by the most astute Earl of Cork, thirteen years later.   They had friends, however, if they had not gear, and no doubt were made much of in the gay Dublin of their time.   The lovely Isabella, Duchess of Rutland, was their fast friend and sympathizer.   One thinks of her protecting the wronged and innocent, for ever fresh and lovely, as Sir Joshua Reynolds painted her ; or as she shines out of a contemporary record at a Rotunda Gardens fête,

in a dress of pink silk with a stomacher and
sleeve-knots of diamonds, and a great hat of
brown velvet, sideways on her charming
powdered head, set with a plume of feathers
and an aigrette of diamonds. Perhaps the
three damsels danced at those Rotunda balls,
for their cousin, the Earl of Grandison, or their
magnificent duchess, would surely never have
allowed them to languish in genteel poverty.

Helen, a woman of spirit, proceeded against
the Duke of Devonshire for the restoration of
their lost acres. But being single-handed and
a woman, she failed, poor soul, and taking her
failure to heart, died of it. I have forgotten
about Elleanora ; but Elizabeth, my Desmond's
grandmother, married a very gallant soldier,
who afterwards was killed at the Battle of
Bunker's Hill. So my Desmond has a lien
with American earth.

If the Duke of Rutland had not taken a
putrid fever after a gay progress through the
North of Ireland, and died of it after a few
days' illness, my sketch need never have been

written. The duchess was so interested in her *protégées* that she had obtained the Duke's promise to settle a handsome pension upon them. No doubt, too, she would have been a powerful friend in any new effort they should make to win back their own. However, the Duke died; the gay days of the Rutland reign were over: her Grace fled back to England a forlorn widow; and there settled on Ireland the black shadow of the approaching Rebellion. And so the wrong went quite unrighted.

That it was acknowledged to a certain extent was shown by the fact that my Desmond's father enjoyed during his lifetime a small State pension, which, however, lapsed with his death.

I can see as I write the grave olive face with the eyes regarding me. What an unsettling thing for a common worker in glass to be lineal descendant of so proud a line! I have said they were Irish princes. They were; in their power, the extent of their territories, and their haughty bearing towards the race from whose

loins they had sprung.   More Irish than the
Irish, such were the Fitzgeralds, alike of
Desmond and Kildare ; but yet no Irish
princes of a half-barbarous magnificence.
Rather with all the stately splendour of the
Courts of the Middle Ages superadded to their
free life ; with traditions of church-building and
college-founding, as you will know, seeing their
remains at Youghal, where is their college, and
the Church of St. Mary's, and the Warden's
House of one magnificent foundation ; and the
town yet landmarked on North and South by
the ruins of the abbeys built by them for
the great mendicant Friars of the Middle
Ages, Franciscan and Dominican.   And
along Blackwater, most lovely of rivers, all
burnished copper and gold in the Autumn
because of the overhanging woods, every high
crag has its castle in ruins, once the proud
eyrie of a Desmond Earl.

The Atlantic roars like wild bulls at the
strand of Youghal.   On the mildest day the
air is full of its thud and reverberation, and

ever a shower of silver spray springs above the strong sea-wall. It must be magnificent in storm. Where the harbour of Youghal narrows to the mouth of Blackwater, one is ferried across to holy Ardmore of St. Declan, with its church and holy well, and St. Declan's stone. Across the ferry is county Waterford. In Ardmore long ago they buried a Desmond Earl; but, exiled from his own Temple-Michael on the Blackwater, his spirit would not rest. So every night, over the breakers and the storm they heard a strange, great voice, crying terribly, "Garoult arointha! arointha,"—which is "Hurry over! Give Gerald a ferry." So at last they took up the unquiet dead, and ferried him to Temple-Michael, where his sleep was sound.

A race of giants certainly. In Youghal streets, ghostly in the autumn weather, what shadows elbow each other! Knights Templars, Desmonds, Elizabethans, Spenser and Raleigh, Noll Cromwell and his Roundheads. The past of Youghal is great and misty, like a huge tapestry blown with the sea-wind, on which stir gigantic figures of knights and horsemen. But of the great and magnifi cent Desmonds remains this—an old man with a wallet of yellow papers, escaped from an irksome trade one hour of a summer day, to pour into the ears of a willing listener his mouldy old tale, at which the well-fed, well-clad world had gaped and shrugged its impertinent shoulders.

MAD MOLLY.

HER cabin is close by a lonely lane that in all its length of miles has not half a dozen human habitations; for a good Irish mile each side there is nothing but the loneliness of winter fields. Just opposite the broken gate leading to her door a bit of road goes between enormously high hedges to the high road—a high road very innocent of traffic, be it said, though occasionally a snorting steam-tram puffs along it. Presently the road winds from its placid level sweep at the foot of the mountains and climbs a steep shelf of the hill into a valley, and disappears through a gorge into the next county. That bye-lane is the eeriest place I know. By Mad Molly's cabin stands a tall stone pine, that in the gloaming looks like a mill chimney. Where the lane and the road meet there is a three-cornered bit of grass, and standing out of it a tall telegraph pole, with an irresistible suggestion of a gibbet.   The place is marshy, and looking down at it of an evening from the higher ground, a stranger will not be persuaded that the solid floor of mist below is not a stretch of water.   The marsh vapours make the strangest effects.   I have walked there of an autumn evening with my heart in my mouth, and needing all my will not to keep looking apprehensively over my shoulder.   I have always companionship ; sometimes human and canine ; more often canine only.   But one could desire no wholesomer company than a fox-terrier, irreverently free from morbidness, and a St. Bernard, very scrupulous as to his duties of guardianship.   By myself nothing would induce me to walk that way—not though it were the goldenest evening summer ever saw—not even in the unwinking noon-light.

The first evening I knew Mad Moll had taken possession of her own cabin, my experience was eerie enough, or rather it was a vicarious experience. I had a friend with me, a girl cramped by the life of cities, and ever eager to stretch her limbs or widen her country sensations. The sun had gone down scarlet in an orange sky. As we walked along, the white smoke of the mist began to exhale from the fields, yellow with old stubble. On one side of the way the fields were clear. On the other side, the mists presently covered them impenetrably. It was as if the fairies were hiding their mysteries from mortal eyes. A wisp of the mist floated across our path; breaths of it came tangling about our feet as we walked. The telegraph pole was full of the voices of the wind; for a minute we did not detect where was the mysterious singing. By the roadside the marshy land emptied its waters into a ditch so deep and wide that it was a miniature pond; under its bushes some disturbance had set up a ghostly suction, a sound of ebb and flow.

I shivered a little as the cabin stood up across the neglected pathway. It looked what

they called it, haunted. It stands on a little
hill—a fairy rath, that no wise human being
would desecrate by his or her intrusion. The
good people did not manifest themselves there
prettily and pleasantly in the only case I know
where they made their presence felt. It was
not an occasion, indeed, for fairy cavalcades or
dances. It proved, too, that though they have
no souls, poor little folk, they are yet friends of
God. It was in a bygone June. The fields
were lush with over-rich grasses; and, like the
Field of the Cloth of Gold, with buttercups and
cowslips. Every hedgerow was a Milky Way
of hawthorn. The cows had just come out of
the city, and were browsing in exquisite con-
tentment amid the silver dews and the delicious
drifts of grass. They were in charge of half a
dozen fellows as reckless and daring as so
many Texan cowboys. It was their first night
to sleep in the haunted house on the fairy rath.
They were playing cards, though, if they had
been out of doors, under the large golden moon,
they might have heard the silver flutes of the

P

fairies.   There was one old reprobate of their number who boasted that he feared not God nor the devil.   He was in bad luck at the cards, and his profanity grew till it displeased even his wild comrades.   They were all clustered, with their heated faces, about the table and its one tallow-candle.   Some who were not playing said afterwards that there was an ominous wind about the house, full of moaning and wailing, and that shadows flitted by the small window, shadows which had no corresponding sub-stance.   Then the gamblers grew quieter, and the sounds outside died away.   But suddenly, at some stroke of ill-luck, this blasphemer broke into a torrent of curses that made his fellows shrink away from him with pale faces.   In the midst of it the cabin door was burst violently open, and what they described afterwards as a howling blast, with sounds of men and horses, drove through the place.   The table and light were over-turned.   The gamblers were down on their faces.   When all was silent again, and some one summoned up courage to light a match, the man who had sworn was dead, suddenly dead as if killed by lightning, but with no cause to show.

I told this story to my companion as we went along—also another tradition of the place : that it was once a pleasant little home among apple-trees, long ago, before the famine of '48 had given Irish vitality a stroke from which it still suffers. A widow and her two rosy-cheeked growing girls lived there. Then there came the time when there was little or no food. Enough potatoes, perhaps, to tide one person over the hard winter, eked out by the few hens and other humble live stock. So the girls, Nora and Katie, made up their minds to go to America, and make a home for the mother there. She would follow them in the spring. The neighbours would be good to her, and she would keep her heart alive in the hope of reunion. They went with prayers and kisses and tears. Perhaps she couldn't have borne to let them go, only the skin was already loose on the faces that had been so plump, and the girls' lips were growing blue with the famine. She could not keep them to become gaunt skeletons like some she had shuddered at. She let them go, drugging herself with dreams of a speedy reunion. Alas! their ship went down in mid-ocean and every soul perished. News came to land by means of a few floating planks, and was spelt out in the village forge by the reader, who was giving less lucky folk the benefit of his learning by translating for them the contents of the papers. Some busybody carried the news to the widow. The sudden telling snapped her sanity. When kind people stole to be with her in her trouble she was gone; the house door open, but of her neither tale nor tidings. For more than forty years no tidings of her had come, and any one who ever thought of her—but those of her own generation were very old—concluded she was long ago with her little girls in the distant country that is heaven.

The stories but excited the interest of my

adventurous friend.   She would peep in at the
broken windows of the haunted house.   At
first she begged for my company, but I had
never been near the place, and should never
dare to brave its memories.   I waited for her
on the road while she lightly ran over the
grass-grown path.   The mist was forming
white walls all about.   In the distance where
the wan sky turned pale as silver, the reflection
below was like a silver mirror.   A tree in the
hedgerow tinkled its leaves like the tinkling of
barley.   The water was sulking somewhere out
of sight.   Suddenly my friend was at my side
with the rapidity of a startled deer.   " Oh,
come away ! " she said, " there's some one,
something, in that awful house."   I didn't need
her dragging me by the hand to run noise-
lessly—as if we feared some unknown terror
hearing our feet in the mist—between the
winding hedgerows, pale with the gold of
withered leaves, till we were in the world
again, the world of inhabited lodges and road-
menders scattering their shingles, and a

solitary ploughman, whose assistance we knew
we could trust to, driving his patient team
up and down the lonely upland.   Then we
leant in view of him over a wall that had
once walled in a quarry, and found our voices.
Peering in at the window she had gazed a
second or two at the place full of shadows,
till she had made out one that looked like a
human shape cowering by what was once
the hearthstone.   She did not look twice,
but fled back to me with her heart in her
mouth.

We were in a mood to believe it anything—
ghost or banshee, or even that most horrible of
Irish spooks, the Watcher by the Ford.   However, a day or two later I heard that old Moll
Donovan had come back.   Where she had
been in the interval God knows—in the pauper
lunatic asylum of some county most probably,
for her gown of blue check looked like a
uniform.   She was quite harmless, poor thing,
as the old neighbours found out presently.
Her mind had stopped short at the hour before

she heard the girls were drowned. Finding
her so harmless, the country people were well-
disposed to take her as in trust from God. They
tidied up the place for her as well as long decay
would permit them, and put in a few sticks of
furniture. She accepted these kind offices
passively, and once installed, kept her cabin
in order. She is a little old woman of between
70 and 80. In her ordinary moods you would
not guess her to be mad, as you see her from
a distance sitting in the sun, her thin hair
decently combed from a patient old face, her
little shawl drawn tightly around bent shoulders.
You would know, though, if you came closer,
and met her wandering eyes. The neighbours
send her a bit of food, enough to keep her
alive, for she does not need much. She calls
the comely and sturdy men and women by the
names of their fathers and mothers, and the
boys and girls are always the boys and girls of
long ago. Not that she is communicative. I
have heard that she rarely speaks, but sits
most of her time in the sun or by her fire-

side crooning over old snatches of songs to herself.

So much for every day and fine weather. In the stormy weather and by moonlight her madness lays hold upon her and drives her out. Perhaps that sulking pool so close to her cabin keeps alive in her crazed memory the thought of the sea that swallowed her darlings. On a wild night by moonlight she is out looking for them. To her every torn pool is the ravening ocean. She flits by one at such a time with all her decent order gone, her scanty hair loose about her face, her eyes full of a devouring question. They say she is still quite harmless, but I am terrified of that apparition gliding by in the shadows. At every ruffled pool she stops, leaning down with anxious scrutiny. She will put her hands to her mouth, trumpet fashion, and holloa, as across the water—"Nora, ahoy!" goes the melancholy cry; "Ahoy, ahoy! Nora, Katie, ahoy! Childher, come home!" Then she listens intently, and hearing nothing but the crying of the wind, roves on again on her ceaseless quest. When this occurs she will wander all night, crying over every pool to the dead girls.

I met her only last night. It was early, but at five o'clock of a November evening the night is already on us. It was nearly full moon, and where the great silver shield was the sky was clear. But westward rose up a dense bank of cloud scudding along to discharge itself in thunderous rain, as the skies had been doing all day. On the murky cloud was a great rainbow, a beautiful perfect arch, silver white as the steady moon-rays poured upon it. I was watching it, heedless for delight, of the storm that was coming up. Suddenly the little dark figure scudded out into the moonlight of the road. She was down on her knees by a troubled pool. "Nora! ahoy! ahoy! Katie, ahoy! Come back, childher! come back!" she went crying, with an intensity of appeal that was agonizing. She was out all night, I suppose, on the plains and the mountains. She will be out many nights this rainy, wintry weather. She will die after some such night of rain and wind. If she were sane, indeed, one such night's wandering would kill her, but the fire of insanity seems to feed life rather than destroy. Kind Father Phil says God will surely give her her reason before she dies. I hope He will, just at the last, when she will know that they are coming to meet her out of a country where is no more sea.

ROSE :

WHEN Rose went away she took with her a sweetness greater than the honey-sweet of the garden-roses. No returning spring or summer brings back that wholesome fragrance. Where are you blooming, Rose ? in which of the manifold gardens of death ? Nay, in no garden, for you were never a garden flower ; but on some high sweet moorland of the Kingdom of Heaven, where, it seems to me, we shall each find our own country, but finer, rarer, and with neither sickness, pain, nor mortality. Rose was like a brave spray of heather, dancing before sun and wind in that open Northern country of hers, which is redolent of the peat-smoke. " My

cluster of nuts," one might call her, emulating
the old poets of Ireland who so-named their
nut-brown mistresses. Her face only ceased
to be brown just below where the hair rippled
nobly off her frank forehead. Bright, sun-
caressed face, white teeth, white forehead ;
they gave her a frankness like an open-faced
boy. Add to these the bravest and most
unstained eyes that ever lit a human face,
and you will perhaps imagine, but dimly, my
Rose.

She was the daughter of a little Northern
farmer, and was born on the eve of St. John,
the night when the fairies are all abroad, and
their revels are lit by leaping fires on every
hill in the country-side. I think, when the
mother slept with the child on her breast, the
most beneficent of all the fairies must have
crept and kissed the baby's cheek, and have
whispered : " Be brave and generous, truthful
and loving, child ; and also have eyes to see
and ears to hear and heart to feel all that is
sweetest and noblest." But who cast in this

fair horoscope the black shadow of an early
death? Not the fairies, for with the great
affairs of life and death they have nothing to
do. Life and death God holds in His hands;
and He alone understands why in her bright
morning of life our Rose should have drooped
and broken on her stalk.

But this was years afterwards. Rose's
mother is a little woman, with as many
wrinkles in her face as a walnut shell. The
father died so long ago that I do not remember
ever to have heard Rose speak of him. For
her growing up there were the exquisite
country pleasures, the long, long summer days
of a child's life, which seems, looking back, to
have been always summer. Rose was the
youngest child, much younger than her two
sisters, and therefore especially a pet. So
many interests there are in a country child's
life, with the lambs, the calves, the fowls, the
water-hen's nest under the osiers in the pond,
and the last brood of downy yellow ducklings,
so pretty that one could gaze all day at their

yellow fluff and black jewels of eyes.   And there is the old orchard, which goes from pink to green, and one day you shall find the green globes of fruit turning rosy on the side next the sun; and the delight, when the reapers are reaping, of finding the first blackberries; and the haymaking time, when one rode home unsteadily on the first great load, and afterwards, in the green evening lit by the white lamp of a moon, disported in the hay; and the mushroom-gathering, when one runs here and there in exquisite excitement over the white heads, and is deceived now by a puff-ball, again by a nodding dog-daisy buried in rank grass.   No wonder the day should be long, being so full, for it is your monotonous, empty days that slip over you like a dream, as it is the monotonous lives slip by unnoted, till some day one finds with a great surprise that one is old, and Death knocking dully at the portal.

But after such days it might well be that Rose would be content to nestle by her mother's skirt on a little creepy stool, and gazing into the dark peat, with its sudden showers of sparks, to listen dreamily to the stories of the fairies in the rath, and of giants and heroes. No hobgoblin tales, however, for the mother was too kind to frighten her wee girl; though I think even then my Rose's well-balanced mind would have selected what was profitable of the stories, and rejected the merely horrible.

There, in the little brown house, Rose grew and throve. She wrote her first little stories in the tangled orchard, and poised her rhymes sitting on the bench by the house-door, from which she afterwards dated a letter : " From the stone bench in the sun, where I sit nursing my little old cough." But then there was no apprehension of coughs, though her father had gone off in a rapid "decline," as the country people call it. In those valleys among the hills it is hard to realize that consumption scourges the tall people; yet it is so. The damps in winter curl heavily in the hollows, and wreathe the hill-brows; and again, there has been so much intermarriage, for though the Church of their allegiance strictly prohibits the marriage of near kin, a whole county will be far-away cousins to each other.

After her convent school, Rose was at home for a little while. She would never have left home if one kindly neighbour could have had his will. He was a man of the North, brave and stalwart, and setting all his heart the way of this thornless Rose; but Rose had nothing for him except that open friendship which was so delightful a quality in her. His hope lasted even to her grave, and it may be beyond it, but she never gave him false hopes of winning her. No man ever quite touched her heart in this way. Among the many men who gave her admiration and devotion she had her preferences, but none warmed to love. Perhaps it was this absence of an engrossing love that enabled her to shine with such a steady light of tenderness on those of us she cared for. With Rose doubt or misunderstanding were impossible. Remembering her genius for friendship, one sighs—

"What a thing friendship is, world without end!"

There were no jealousies or bickerings or hurts of any kind in one's friendship with Rose. Yet on all the world outside she shone with such a wide impartial light of kindness and tolerance that one is tempted to say of Rose that, like the sun, she shone on the just and the unjust.

After that little time at home she drifted to the city—nay, not drifted, for she came with a steady purpose. Her clever fingers worked with her brain, and her untaught sketches were full of promise. In Dublin she entered as an art student, and there began the friendships which sweetened her latter years. Literary folk, artists, politicians; her circle widened as wide as the circles of the sea, and took in many whom she had worshipped from afar off. Of these there was one to whom she was able to give sweet service. He, too, lived under the roof of the kind woman who was Rose's

Q

hostess. He had been in prison long years for his Fenianism, and was the gentlest soul of all those who took up arms in a forlorn attempt to free their country. He was a poet and a dreamer, with a man's heroic bravery and a woman's softness and purity. He came from prison stone-deaf, and with the dullest glimmer of sight between his eyelids. To him Rose devoted herself. To him she became eyes and ears, and chained herself to his invalid's couch with a strong delight in rendering service to one who had so greatly dared and suffered. For him she learned the deaf-and-dumb alphabet, at which she became very 'proficient; and when I desire to recall my Rose at her sweetest and brightest, I conjure up a picture of her flashing the words from her fingers, her dear cheeks colouring and paling, her eyes full of bright questioning, as I once saw her interpreting for a deaf friend of later years. Her service to her friend lasted during two winters and a summer. In the early part of the second summer he died; the deaf heard and the blind saw. He died with Rose kneeling by his head. His last half-inarticulate words were of God, of Ireland, and of Rose.

After that, veering between Dublin and Tyrone, Rose lived and loved, and wrought her delicate stories and poems. Finally she settled in Dublin, and became one of a little set of bookish and artistic people. Folk were enchanted with her fresh naturalness; she had the beauty of a lovely peasant with the added charm of cultivation of mind and heart. Those were days of prosperity for this Rose. She went hither and thither, taking the joy of her youth and living every hour of her waking life. She was ever well and normal in mood. As editor of the children's department of a large weekly newspaper, she had a delightful office; crimson blinds behind lace curtains, brilliant Japanese fans and gay pictures; a roaring fire behind a picture screen, and in the midst of this warmth—Rose. One stepped out of the winter streets into Rose's sanctum, and winter was flown; and there stood Rose ready to take one's fardel of troubles, and, blowing on the unsubstantial things, laugh them away into air and mist.

Alack! the gay days. One never-to-be-forgotten Christmas, when the streets were full of murk, Rose heard from Tyrone that the beloved little mother was ill and longed for her. The wise physician who was Rose's attached friend, and had watched over her lest in her, too, the seeds of "the decline" should appear, in vain tried to keep her. Her love sent her on the long railway journey in the damp December day. She returned with a heavy cold, caught on the journey down. The remainder of that winter and the following summer she had varying health, and after an absence I just came back in time to see her before she went to Arcachon for sure recovery. I said good-bye to her one November evening, in a little house by the sea. Afterwards I remembered that the last words were all of *my* concerns. The brave reticence was with her to the last; I suppose to her, as to other

people, it would be easier to face the night of
death with a warm hand in hers, but, instead,
she closed upon herself the door of life, and
with her face to the storm, and her heart
uplifted to God, stepped out on the drear way
she must walk alone.

Arcachon proved but an added pain. A cruel
winter withered all the South, and the Southern
folk, unused to frost and snow, lit up starveling
fires that were but a mockery of warmth. The
home-hunger, too, ached in the heart of this
untravelled traveller. From the inhospitable
South she went home to the North with the
swallows. We who did not know how ill she
was, clamoured for her return. She bade us
wait till she was better. We waited through
the fresh spring and summer, and while the
pale autumn darkened to winter. In the
winter she died, quite without warning to us,
in the morning of life, like herself. I am not
sure that there was not some cruelty in that
she would not trust us with the heavy secret,
but should let us be wounded some day with

that sorrowful news in the blind columns of a newspaper. However, she thought it right, and she was not one, like me, to make and unmake her judgments of right and wrong ten times a minute.

She sleeps on the sunny side of an old Tyrone churchyard, among the saints, and in a spot which she chose herself while she had yet six months of life. They asked me once to come and see the room where she died, and her grave covered thick with primroses; but I would not go. I saw nothing of her slow dying, and to me she is still as one living, though she comes not nor speaks out of the silence.

A VILLAGE PRIEST.

HIS house stood as formal as a toy house in a Noah's Ark amid patches of grass, grey with sea-sand. It was very new, and built of dreary yellow brick. There were no flowers about. What flower. would thrive indeed in this valley of wind-blown sand? His was the one house of consideration, for the people were so poor that even the meanest public-house could find no customers. The homes of his parishioners were high on the steep walls of the vale, ragged things, clinging like last year's nests on a storm-swept bough. His house was the nearest to the sea, that was out there beyond the lines of yellow sand. The sound of it was in the air. Lonely as the place was on an April day, one shuddered to imagine it of a

November evening; nature was so tremendous there and humanity so little. The great and awful Heads rose like a gigantic wall against the sky, and ever their stony faces gazed out to sea away from the stunted figures of men moving about their base.

His cure was a wide one. The valley ran for some miles inland; five miles they said it measured, and it was dotted along its course by the curious little pillars which marked a saint's stations. If he wore his knees from one of those stones to another he was indeed saintly. One entered the oblong gash in the land climbing over a high hill's edge, and then tumbling precipitously down the steep ravine, in imminent danger of breaking the horse's knees and one's own neck. It is an experience to be gone through at first with your heart in your mouth, but after a score of escapes you begin to trust in your star and the sure-footed mountain ponies. At the foot of the descent a bridge crossed a little river singing on its way from the hills to the sea. Here the cabins clustered most thickly. In one or two a blear-eyed man came to the door to look at us, and we could see through the thick smoke within an old-fashioned weaver's loom. Weaving has been their industry from time immemorial, but with so many hindrances: for first there is a scarcity of yarn, and then the looms are so unreliable, and the cloth once spun, it is so very, very far to the market, that they can scarcely be said to thrive out of their weaving. There were no children playing in the gutter, as one usually sees them in an Irish village. The few we saw at the doorsteps were dirty and pallid. The fowls croaked complainingly of how hard it was to pick up a living. The only cheerful things were the adorable mountain lambs, that, with wee black faces of a mingled innocence and sagacity, trotted by us with the tameness of a dog.

Down in the valley one was out of the world. The weaver folk only spoke the Irish, and we had no interpreters. As we made our way to the priest's house, we had to spring from one spit of sand to another, for the ground was threaded by devious little streams making their way to the sea. The water was stained red with the iron ore of which the mountains are full.

We came opportunely, for as we approached the square, ugly dwelling, we saw coming towards us, from another side, a tall, slender clerical figure, which, as it came, leaped stone walls and streamlets with a surprising agility. Its owner came up to us hat in hand, a smile on his lean dark face. The priest was quite a young man, twenty-seven at the outside. We knew at once that he was very glad to see us, so glad that he scarcely listened to our reasons for coming. He stood mechanically stroking the head of the retriever that followed at his heels, with the kind, wintry smile on his melancholy mouth. The smile really lit up his face palely, as you may see winter sunlight brightening all the bare fields. Presently he preceded us courteously into his house.

The room into which he led us had two large

undraped windows. The floor was uncarpeted, but very clean. There was no sign of the tobacco with which a lonely man might some-times companion himself. A crucifix on the mantleshelf, a couple of pious pictures on the wall, a bookcase of theological works, most unprofitable to the lay person, and in a corner a few ordinary books, novels, and the like, were the adornments. Some hard chairs and a square centre-table were all the furniture. He apologized for his novels with a deprecatory smile—the follies of his student days, he said, but we noticed that they were dog's-eared and thumbed far more than Suarez and Liguori.

After he had given some whispered orders to his bare-foot maid servant he volunteered to show us something of the glen. We sallied forth, facing the enormous Heads that seemed to shut away the world. We went up to a weaver's cottage in their shadow, wading and climbing half the time. The old weaver and the young weaver, his son, showed us how the loom worked, while a red-shawled girl sat with her bent head against the little square window singing low to her spinning-wheel. The interior of the cottage was dense with smoke that smarted in our eyes, and made us cough vigorously. One wondered how they lived in the atmosphere, but they seemed to mind it little, nor did the priest, who stood and interpreted for us.

On our way back he led us to talk of many things—politics, art, books, society. He put to us many leading questions in his soft, slow voice. A great eagerness brightened up his face, that was at once innocent and sad. He had in his mind a curious hotch-potch of information. He was like the nuns in a convent school I well knew, some of whom had not read a newspaper since they came into the convent, and who believed that the world had since stood still.

When he returned to his house he showed us a photograph of his home, a long, low farmhouse, with an abundance of flowers. Before he door stood the farmer himself, in the familiar attitude, his arm on his pony's neck. His wife sat on a stone seat in the sun, with white ringlets under a be-ribboned cap, and her hands folded demurely in her lap.

"It is so long since I have seen them," sighed the priest wistfully. " O no ; it was not that they were so far away—only in the next county ; but here, where there was no railroad, nor even mail-cars, travelling was so expensive." We said something of the pretty house. He sighed his acquiescence. " Ah, yes, very pretty ; and smothered in flowers. And that country all velvet green, with a salmon river, and woods on the horizon, and far away the blue hills so mild against the sky. Now here one could not grow a flower ; there is only the heather, and the little rock mosses. A rose-tree my mother sent was blown beyond recall last winter, and since I have not tried to rear flowers." He said it as out of utter home-sickness. Afterwards he told us it was five years since he had seen his father or mother.

Presently we sat down to a bit of roast

mutton, flanked by the temperate tea. As he uncovered the meat he rubbed his hands with mild satisfaction. By the merest chance he had fresh meat to-day of all days, and like most people beyond reach of a market he over-estimated the dainty. As we talked over the meal he became very frank. The poor priest was full of aspirations after literature and art— indeed his notions were somewhat crude as to what these included. He took with great pride the top paper from a heap in the corner. It was a London Sunday paper. He beamed at us deprecatingly. "You see I get a little of everything in this," he said, "so that I am not out of the world."

He told us something of the isolation in which he lived. There was not an English-speaking person nearer than six Irish miles away. He knew only so much of the Irish as enabled him to get along with his people. There was not one to exchange an idea with him. His flock, so poor and wretched, were atrophied in mind as in body. "These good friends keep me from madness," he said, pointing to the books, "in the winter when the sea is roaring with a thunder that fills all the Glen, and the Heads shut out the grey sky." He beamed at the shabby covers. " I don't get tired of them," he said, "as you young ladies, living in the world, might imagine. They are such good books, and full of information as well as amusement." This last with an innocently apologetic air.

He told us so much of his daily life that we could picture it. He had enormously long walks to visit his flock. There were many sick calls, for vitality in the Glen was low, and consumption, and all the forms of chest disease scourged the under-fed people. Mental diseases too were common, and the county supposed to furnish an extraordinary large percentage of the madness of the entire island. The priest had theories on the subject. It was partly due to the irritation of the brain caused by much fish-eating, for at times of the year the people exist entirely on fish ; partly to the intermarriages, for these people had married in their own county since the Cromwellian planters drove them there from the fertile lowlands, and relationships amongst them were practically inextricable; partly too, no doubt, to the place, with its extreme humidity and loneliness.

"I fear the madness myself," said our poor priest, his face relapsing to its old unlit melancholy, "for there is always the famine coming. It was here last year, and the year before, and will be here this year. Famine! Indeed, except for the time when the boats can put out, they are always famine-stricken. And always there is the low fever bred by starvation, in the Glen. But the thing that haunts me is the big famine that will come some day, when all the Glen will die of starvation. Year after year we have had help just in the nick of time. But what if the help should come late? This year, or next year! God forgive me for fearing it, but it haunts me all night and every night, and when I go my long walks through

the Glen." As he told us his long-contained
fears, the sweat came on his forehead in big
beads. " I pray hard," he said again, "against
the madness that may come to me of loneliness
and the fear for my people. Perhaps such
despair is a temptation from the devil, but
what if God had destined us in the Glen for
martyrdom ? " He looked at us with dilated
eyes, and we felt that we understood then the
profound and terrible melancholy of his face.

Poor priest! So kind and gentle and
hospitable. As we left him, the melancholy
that had lifted, settled down on his face. His
breviary was under his arm, his stick in his
hand, the dog, his one friend, rubbing himself
insinuatingly against the black cassock. He
was going one of his long tramps to visit a sick
girl. He would not return till the evening
was settled down on the Glen, where it comes
early, for the mountains and the Heads blot
out the sky. So human in his sympathies, with
his pathetic intellectual longings ; how long
before another companionable spirit came to

R

his Glen at the end of the world? I often think of him in his loneliness, and shall think with more acute sympathy when winter has settled grayly on the Glen.

THE END.

Woodfall & Kinder, Printers, 70 to 76, Long Acre, London, W.C.

November, 1893.

MESSRS.
LAWRENCE & BULLEN'S

List of Publications.

LONDON:

16, HENRIETTA STREET, COVENT GARDEN

CONTENTS.

ALPHABETICAL LIST

OF

LAWRENCE & BULLEN'S PUBLICATIONS.

ALLEN, GRANT.— SCIENCE IN ARCADY.
Crown 8vo. 5*s.*
> "Holiday papers of a naturalist. The love of the country is in them all."—*Speaker.*

ANACREON.—The Greek Text, with THOMAS STANLEY'S Translation. Edited by A. H. BULLEN. Illustrated by J. R. WEGUELIN. Fcap. 4to. £1 1*s. net.*

ANDERSEN, HANS CHRISTIAN. — THE LITTLE MERMAID, AND OTHER STORIES. Translated by R. NISBET BAIN. With 65 Illustrations (chiefly full-page) by J. R. WEGUELIN. Royal 4to. 12*s.* 6*d.*

> * Also 150 copies on hand-made paper, with the illustrations mounted on Japanese paper.

BARRETT, C. R. B.—ESSEX: HIGHWAYS, BY-WAYS, AND WATERWAYS. First and Second Series. Written and Illustrated by C. R. B. BARRETT. (With 18 full-page etchings, and upwards of 200 drawings.) 2 vols. 12*s.* 6*d. net* per volume.

> * 120 copies on fine paper, with additional etchings. Price £1 11*s.* 6*d. net* per volume.
> "An excellent and original work."—*Athenæum.*

BARRETT, C. R. B.—A HISTORY OF THE TRINITY HOUSE OF DEPTFORD STROND. 12s. 6d. *net.*

BARRETT, C. R. B.—ILLUSTRATED GUIDES.
1. SOUTHWOLD. *6d.*   2. ALDEBURGH. *6d.*
3. St. OSYTH, WIVENHOE, FINGRINGHOE, and BRIGHTLINGSEA. *6d.*
· 4. SOUTHEND, HADLEIGH, ROCHFORD, &c. *6d.*
5. IPSWICH, HARWICH, &c. *6d.*
6. GREAT YARMOUTH, *6d.*   7. CAISTER CASTLE, *3d.*
8. St. OSYTH PRIORY, *3d.*   9. COLCHESTER, *6d.*

"Carefully written, well printed, and amply illustrated.—*Manchester Guardian.*

BECKFORD, WILLIAM. — VATHEK. Edited by DR. RICHARD GARNETT. With 8 full-page Etchings by HERBERT NYE. Demy 8vo. £1 1s. *net.*

* 600 copies printed for England and America. Also 70 copies on Japanese vellum, with an additional etching.

BOCCACCIO, GIOVANNI. — THE DECAMERON. Translated by JOHN PAYNE. Illustrated by LOUIS CHALON. 2 vols. Imp. 8vo. £3 3s. *net.* (With 20 full-page Illustrations.)

* 1,000 copies printed for England and America.

BULLEN, A. H.—ANTHOLOGIES.
LYRICS FROM ELIZABETHAN SONG-BOOKS. Revised edition. Fcp. 8vo. 5s.

LYRICS FROM ELIZABETHAN DRAMATISTS. Revised edition. Fcp. 8vo. 5s.

BULLEN, A. H.—ANTIENT DROLLERIES, in Six Parts. 3s. 6d. per Part *net.*

> * Parts I, II, and III. " Cobbe's Prophecies," " Pymlico, or Runne Redcap," and " Quips upon Questions," have appeared. Other Parts are in active preparation. The edition consists of 300 copies.

CATULLUS.—Edited by S. G. Owen, Senior Student of Christ Church. Illustrated by J. R. Weguelin. Fcp. 4to. 16s. *net.*

> * Also 110 copies on Japanese vellum, with an additional illustration. Price £1 11s. 6d. *net.*

CHURCHILL, CHARLES.—ROSCIAD. Edited, with an Introduction and Notes, by Robert W. Lowe. With Portraits. Royal 4to. £1 1s. *net.*

> * The edition consists of 400 numbered copies.
>
> "The edition is not only good, but magnificent."— *Guardian.*

CHURCHILL, CHARLES. — PORTFOLIO OF PORTRAITS. 25s. *net.*

CRANE, WALTER.—CLAIMS OF DECORATIVE ART. Fcp. 4to. 7s. 6d. *net.*

> " No one has a better right than Mr. Walter Crane to write about the *Claims of Decorative Art,* for he is certainly one of the best masters of decorative design whom we have had among us for many a long day. . . . The book is admirably ' got up,' and does credit to the publishers."— *World.*

D'AULNOY, MADAME.—FAIRY TALES. Newly Translated into English, with an Introduction by ANNE THACKERAY RITCHIE, and Illustrations by CLINTON PETERS. Fcp. 4to. 7s. 6d.

> "An admirable gift book for girls and boys."— *National Observer.*
>
> "An exceedingly pleasing Volume." — *Saturday Review.*
>
> * *Prospectus*, with specimen plate, on application.

DAVIDSON, JOHN. — SENTENCES AND PARAGRAPHS. 18mo. 3s. 6d.

EARLE, A. M.— CHINA - COLLECTING IN AMERICA. With Illustrations. Fcp. 4to. 16s.

EDMONDS, MRS.—THE HISTORY OF A CHURCH MOUSE. A modern Greek story. Crown 8vo. 1s. 6d.

> "A graceful story, and one, moreover, which incidentally throws considerable light on the manners and customs of the Greek peasants in the more sequestered regions of that beautiful country at the present time." — *Speaker.*

GIFT, THEO.—FAIRY TALES FROM THE FAR EAST, Illustrated by O. VON GLEHN. Fcp. 4to. 5s.

> 'A charming volume adapted from the 'Birth Stories of Buddha,' as Englished by Professor Rhys Davies, with admirable drawings by Otto von Glehn."—*Saturday Review.*

GIFT, THEO.—AN ISLAND PRINCESS. A novel. 1 vol. Crown 8vo. 5s.

GISSING, GEORGE.—THE ODD WOMEN. A novel. 3 vols. 31s. 6d.

GISSING, GEORGE.—DENZIL QUARRIER. A novel. 1 vol. 6s.

GISSING, GEORGE.—THE EMANCIPATED. A novel. 1 vol. 6s. [*New and cheaper Edition.*

HARRADEN, BEATRICE.—SHIPS THAT PASS IN THE NIGHT. A novel. 1 vol. Crown 8vo. 3s. 6d. [*Fourth Edition.*

JÓKAI, MAURUS.—EYES LIKE THE SEA. A Romance. Translated from the Hungarian by R. NISBET BAIN. 3 vols. Crown 8vo. 31s. 6d.

KNIGHT, JOSEPH.—THEATRICAL NOTES (1874–1880). A contribution towards the History of the Modern English Stage. Demy 8vo. 6s.

   * Also 250 large-paper copies, with portraits of eminent actors and actresses.

LINTON, W. J.—EUROPEAN REPUBLICANS. Recollections of Mazzini and his Friends. Demy 8vo. 10s. 6d.

   " The book is one that cannot be read without some amount of searching of heart, for however our range of

view, our political instincts have developed since '48, it
would to-day be hard to find (save perhaps among the
Russian and Polish exiles) so single-minded, unselfish, and
devoted a band of politicians as these men, whom Mr.
Linton revered in their lives and has fitly honoured after
their death."—*Manchester Guardian.*

LINTON, W. J.—THE FLOWER AND THE
STAR, and other Stories for Children. Written
and Illustrated by W. J. LINTON. Fcp. 8vo.
3*s.* 6*d.*

" Delightfully fresh and unaffected. . . . The beautiful little woodcuts by the author form the most appropriate
and expressive illustrations of such simple and pleasing
stories that could be desired.—*Saturday Review.*

LINTON, W. J. — CATONINETALES. A
Domestic Epic, by HATTIE BROWN, a young
lady of colour lately deceased at the age of 14.
Edited and Illustrated by W. J. LINTON.
Demy 8vo.   7*s.* 6*d. net.*   (330 copies printed.)

"The cat in the bag, on p. 48, though small, is too
terrible."—*Saturday Review.*

MISCELLANIES—Bibliographical and Historical.
THE   DIALOGUS   OR   COMMUNYNG
BETWIXT THE WYSE KING SALOMON
AND MARCOLPHUS. Reproduced in fac-
simile by the Oxford University Press from the
unique copy of the edition printed by GERARD
LEEU about 1492.   Edited by E. GORDON

DUFF. Small 4to. 10*s*. 6*d. net.* (350 copies printed.)

"Mr. Duff's edition possesses in a singular degree all the qualities which are necessary to justify a facsimile reprint."—*Guardian.*

ANTONIO DE GUARAS; 'OR, THE ACCESSION OF QUEEN MARY : being the Contemporary Narrative of Antonio de Guaras, a Spanish Merchant resident in London. Edited, with an Introduction, by RICHARD GARNETT, LL.D. Sm. 4to. 10*s*. 6*d. net.* (350 copies printed.)

"On the interest and importance of the narrative itself it is needless to dwell. . . . It is equally needless to say that Dr. Garnett has discharged his functions as editor in a masterly fashion."—*Times.*

SEX QUAM ELEGANTISSIME EPISTOLE IMPRESSE PER WILLELUM CAXTON ET DILIGENTER EMENDATE PER PETRUM CARMELIANUM. Reproduced in facsimile by JAMES HYATT. Edited, with a Translation, by GEORGE BULLEN, C.B., LL.D. Sm. 4to. 10*s*. 6*d. net.* (350 copies printed.)

"As a specimen of Caxtonian typography—and, we may add, of its artistic reproduction by means of photographic lithography—no less than on account of Dr. Bullen's exegetic labours, this reprint will be accounted curious and valuable."—*Times.*

INFORMACŌN FOR PYLGRYMES : Reproduced in facsimile by the Oxford University

Press from the unique copy preserved in the
Advocates' Library at Edinburgh. Edited by
E. GORDON DUFF. Sm. 4to. 10s. 6d. net.
(350 copies printed.)

  * A prospectus of the *Miscellanies* will be sent on
application.

MUSES' LIBRARY—

POEMS OF WILLIAM BROWNE, OF
TAVISTOCK. Edited by GORDON GOODWIN,
with an Introduction by A. H. BULLEN. 2 vols
18mo. 10s. net.

POEMS OF WILLIAM BLAKE. Edited by
W. B. YEATS. 1 vol. 18mo. 5s. net.

POEMS OF JOHN DONNE. Edited by E.
K. CHAMBERS, with an Introduction by GEORGE
SAINTSBURY. 2 vols. 18mo. 10s. net.

VOLUMES OF THE SERIES ALREADY ISSUED.

WORKS OF ROBERT HERRICK. Edited
by A. W. POLLARD. With a Preface by A. C.
SWINBURNE. 2 vols. 18mo. 10s. net.

POEMS AND SATIRES OF ANDREW
MARVELL. Edited by G. A. AITKEN. 2 vols.
18mo. 10s. net.

POEMS OF EDMUND WALLER. Edited
by G. THORN DRURY. 1 vol. 18mo. 5s. net.

POEMS OF JOHN GAY. Edited by J
UNDERHILL. 2 vols. 18mo. 10s. net.

  * Also 200 large-paper copies.
  † Other volumes of the series are in active preparation.

O'NEILL, MOIRA.—AN EASTER VACATION. A story. Crown 8vo. 3*s.* 6*d.*

ORME, TEMPLE. — MATRICULATION CHEMISTRY. Small 8vo. 2*s.* 6*d.*

ORME, TEMPLE.—RUDIMENTS OF CHEMISTRY. Small 8vo. 2*s.* 6*d.*

OWEN, J. A. (Editor of "On Surrey Hills," &c.) FOREST, FIELD AND FELL. Crown 8vo. 3*s.* 6*d.*

PEARCE, J. H. (Author of "Esther Pentreath," &c.) DROLLS FROM SHADOWLAND. 18mo. 3*s.* 6*d.*

POWELL, G. H.—OCCASIONAL RHYMES AND REFLECTIONS. Demy 8vo. Boards, 1*s.* 6*d.* Cloth, 2*s.*

"Mr. Powell may fairly claim to share with Mr. Traill the laurels of modern English pasquinade."—*Times.*

PRIDEAUX, MISS S. T.—HISTORICAL SKETCH OF BOOKBINDING. (With a chapter "ON STAMPED BINDINGS," by E. GORDON DUFF.) Sm. 4to. 6*s. net.*

* Also 120 copies (numbered) on fine paper, with two facsimiles specially prepared ·by Mr. Griggs. £1 1*s. net.*

"We propose to consider the subject as it falls naturally into three main periods : the first from 1494, when Aldus Manutius had his printing press at Venice, to the end of the 16th century. This was the period of Maioli and Grolier, of the royal bindings done for Francis I. and Henri II. The art attained almost at once its highest perfection, at all events from the point of view of

design. Secondly, the 17th century, with which are
associated the names of the Eves and Le Gascon.
Thirdly, the 18th century, the time of Boyat, Duseuil,
Nicolas, and Antoine Padeloup and the Deromes, in
France, and of the Harleian style and Roger Payne in
England. Any division must necessarily be somewhat
arbitrary, but it happens that in this case the centuries
correspond pretty definitely to the different types of the
art at different periods of its development."

RABELAIS, FRANCIS. — THE WORKS OF MASTER FRANCIS RABELAIS. Translated by Sir THOMAS URQUHART, of Cromarty, and PETER ANTONY MOTTEUX. With an Introduction by ANATOLE DE MONTAIGLON. Illustrated by L. CHALON. 2 vols. Imp. 8vo. £3 3s. net.

1,000 copies for England and America.

* *Prospectus*, with specimen plate, will be sent on
application.

The copious racy vocabulary of Urquhart's "Rabelais," the odd quirks and flourishes, the gusto and swing
of the rollicking narrative, can never fail to delight liberal
readers.

The publishers of the present edition claim to have
dealt handsomely with Rabelais and Sir Thomas
Urquhart. They invited a very distinguished French
artist, Mons. L. Chalon, to paint a series of oil-colour
illustrations, which have been reproduced by Dujardin.
The originals were lately exhibited at the " Blanc et Noir,
Paris, where they were awarded a First Medal.

Prefixed to the translation is an essay on Rabelais
(specially written for this edition) by a scholar of European
reputation, M. Anatole de Montaiglon, whose knowledge
of early French literature is certainly unsurpassed and
probably unequalled. Facsimiles of rare title-pages of
early French editions accompany the Introduction.

The volumes are printed by Messrs. Whittingham in
the best style of the Chiswick Press.

ROBERTS, MORLEY.—KING BILLY OF BALLARAT, and other Tales. Crown 8vo. 5s.

" Mr. Roberts is a capital story-teller, with an incisive and dramatic style that is thoroughly individual.—*Saturday Review.*

ROBERTS, MORLEY.—SONGS OF ENERGY. Square 16mo. 5s.

ROBERTS, MORLEY.—LAND-TRAVEL AND SEA-FARING. With Illustrations by A. D. McCORMICK. Demy 8vo. 7s. 6d.

ROBERTS, MORLEY.—THE MATE OF THE VANCOUVER. Crown 8vo. 3s. 6d.

ROBERTS, CECIL.—ADRIFT IN AMERICA; OR, WORK AND ADVENTURE IN THE STATES. Edited by MORLEY ROBERTS. Demy 8vo. 5s.

ROBINSON, H. J. — COLONIAL CHRONO-LOGY: A chronology of the principal events connected with the English Colonies and India, from the close of the fifteenth century to the present time. With Maps. Crown folio. 16s.

"Nothing but cordial praise can be given to this valuable book."—*Manchester Guardian.*

" The book is one which ought to find a place in every library of reference."—*Speaker.*

"Admirably arranged on a plan equally simple and comprehensive."—*World.*

* *Prospectus* will be sent on application.

RUSSIAN FAIRY TALES.—Translated by R. NISBET BAIN. Illustrated by C. M. GERE Demy 8vo. 5s.   [*Second edition.*

" The very best fairy-book that we have seen this year (or indeed for many years). . . . The six admirable full-page illustrations to ' Russian Fairy Tales,' by C. M. Gere (a name quite new to us by the way), approach as near to our ideal fairy-book pictures as may be. Messrs. Lawrence & Bullen are to be congratulated on having produced the most delightful story-book of the season."— *Daily Chronicle.*

" A book to read and a book to keep.—*Pall Mall Gazette.*

" Delightfully original, naïve and humorous."— *Truth.*

SCARRON, PAUL, COMICAL WORKS. Done into English by TOM BROWN of Shifnal. With an Introduction by J. J. JUSSERAND. Illustrated from the Designs of OUDRY. 2 vols. Demy 8vo. £1 1s. *net.*

* Also 150 copies on Japanese vellum. £2 2s. *net.*

" Published in a handsome form with every luxury of type and paper. A special feature consists in the designs by Oudry, the famous dog-painter to Louis XV. These are masterpieces of spirit and taste. . . . To the knowledge elsewhere accessible concerning the book, M. Jusserand now adds a brilliant account of the author." —*Athenæum.*

STRANG, WILLIAM. — DEATH AND THE PLOUGHMAN'S WIFE. A Ballad. With 9 Etchings and 2 Mezzotint Engravings. Folio.

* The price and the number of copies will be announced shortly.

TOLD IN THE VERANDAH.—Passages in the Life of Colonel Bowlong, set down by his Adjutant. Crown 8vo. 3*s*. 6*d*.

[*Third edition.*

"Colonel Bowlong is a liar of the first water. He recks not whether he deals with tiger-stories or with his alleged noble deeds on the field of battle. His tiger-story is one of the best we have ever read."—*St. James's Gazette.*

BY THE AUTHOR OF "TOLD IN THE VERANDAH." — A BLACK PRINCE AND OTHER STORIES. Crown 8vo. 3*s*. 6*d*.

TYNAN, KATHARINE. — A CLUSTER OF NUTS. Crown 8vo. 3*s*. 6*d*.

VANBRUGH, SIR JOHN.—WORKS. Edited by W. C. WARD. 2 vols. Demy 8vo. (With a Portrait.) £1 5*s*. *net*.

WALLIS, HENRY.—PERSIAN AND ORIENTAL CERAMIC ART. Parts. I. and II. Folio. 14*s*. *net*.

WELLS, CHARLES.—STORIES AFTER NATURE. With a Preface by W. J. LINTON. Fcp. 8vo. 7*s*. 6*d*. *net*.

* The edition consists of 400 numbered copies.

"The tales, with all their rouge and frippery of form, breathe a singularly clear and upright morality, and are rich in examples of noble manhood and gracious womanhood."—*Athenæum.*

WILLS, C. J.—JOHN SQUIRE'S SECRET. A novel. 1 vol. 3*s*. 6*d*. [*New and cheaper edition.*

YEATS, W. B.—THE CELTIC TWILIGHT. 18mo. 3*s*. 6*d*.

Books published at £3 3s. net.
BOCCACCIO's *Decameron.* 2 vols.
URQUHART'S *Rabelais.* 2 vols.

3-Vol. Novels at £1 11s. 6d.
G. GISSING'S *Odd Women.*
JÓKAI's *Eyes Like the Sea.*

£1 5s. net.
VANBRUGH'S *Plays.* 2 vols.
PORTRAITS ILLUSTRATING
CHURCHILL'S *Rosciad.*

£1 1s. net.
ANACREON. | BECKFORD'S *Vathek.*
CHURCHILL'S *Rosciad.*
PAUL SCARRON.

16s. net.
CATULLUS.

16s.
ROBINSON's *Colonial Chronology.*
EARLE's *China Collecting.*

14s. net.
PARTS I. and II. OF WALLIS'S
Oriental Ceramic Art.

12s. 6d. net.
BARRETT'S *Essex.*
BARRETT'S *Trinity House.*

12s. net.
ANDERSEN, HANS. *Little Mermaid.*

10s. 6d. net.
SALOMON AND MARCOLPHUS.
ANTONIO DE GUARAS.
SEX QUAM ELEGANTISSIME EPIS-
TOLE.
INFORMACŌN FOR PYLGRYMES.

10s. 6d.
LINTON's *European Republicans.*

7s. 6d. net.
LINTON's *Catoninetales.*
WELLS' *Stories After Nature.*
WALTER CRANE'S *Decorative Art.*

7s. 6d.
D'AULNOY's *Fairy Tales.*
MORLEY ROBERTS' *Land Travel.*

6s. net.
MISS PRIDEAUX's *Bookbinding.*

6s.
GISSING, G., *Denzil Quarrier.*
„   „   *The Emancipated.*
KNIGHT's *Theatrical Notes.*

5s. net per Volume.
WILLIAM BROWNE, of Tavistock.
WILLIAM BLAKE. | JOHN DONNE.
JOHN GAY. | ROBERT HERRICK.
ANDREW MARVELL.
EDMUND WALLER.

5s.
GRANT ALLEN's *Science in Arcady.*
BULLEN, A. H. *Lyrics from Song-
Books.*
BULLEN, A. H. *Lyrics from
Dramatists.*
GIFT, THEO. *Fairy Tales.*
„   „   *An Island Princess.*
ROBERTS, MORLEY. *King Billy.*
ROBERTS, C. *Adrift in America.*

3s. 6d. net per Part.
Ancient Drolleries.

3s. 6d.
DAVIDSON's *Sentences.*
HARRADEN's *Ships That Pass.*
LINTON's *Flower and the Star.*
O'NEILL's *Easter Vacation.*
OWEN, J. A., *Woodland Ways.*
PEARCE's *Drolls from Shadowland.*
ROBERTS' *Mate of Vancouver.*
"*Told in the Verandah.*"
"*A Black Prince.*"
TYNAN, KATHARINE. *A Cluster
of Nuts.*
WILLS' *John Squire's Secret.*
YEATS' *Celtic Twilight.*

2s. 6d.
ORME'S *Rudiments of Chemistry.*
„   *Matriculation.*

1s. 6d.
EDMONDS, MRS., *Church Mouse.*
POWELL, G. H., *Rhymes.*

6d. and 3d.
BARRETT's *Illustrated Guides.*

www.ingramcontent.com/pod-product-compliance
Lightning Source LLC
Chambersburg PA
CBHW030637030726
47497CB00006B/1835